WILL KEEN, INDIAN SCOUT

Will Keen lives in two different worlds — one white, one Paiute Indian. He guides wagon trains into Oregon Territory, braving savage lands and equally savage men — of all races — who prey on innocent wagon families. After a decade in the job, Will has no idea that his future will take a different turn with his current assignment. Badly injured after fending off an attempted robbery, he must teach a young woman, Sarah, how to guide the train. Love blossoms between them — but an outlaw is hell-bent on revenge . . .

ART ISBERG

WILL KEEN, INDIAN SCOUT

Complete and Unabridged

LINFORD
Leicester

First published in Great Britain in 2017 by
Robert Hale
an imprint of The Crowood Press
Wiltshire

First Linford Edition
published 2020
by arrangement with
The Crowood Press
Wiltshire

A catalogue record for this book is available
from the British Library.

ISBN 978–1–4448–4532–7

Published by
Ulverscroft Limited
Anstey, Leicestershire

Set by Words & Graphics Ltd.
Anstey, Leicestershire
Printed and bound in Great Britain by
T. J. International Ltd., Padstow, Cornwall

This book is printed on acid-free paper

1

Will Keen reined his horse to a halt on the rim of a vast canyon complex sloping away downhill before him. As far as the eye could see, treeless, stone-topped mesas and bare rock cliffs rose high above the sombre grey of sagebrush flats interspersed with sudden streaks of bone-white sulphur. A gust of hot wind borne on the mid-day heat spawned a twisting dust devil dancing across flats like a white ghost, only to die and disappear as quick as it was born.

Will twisted in the saddle looking back across undulating brushlands to the distant blink of twenty-three canvas-topped Conestoga wagons still five miles behind. They barely seemed to move, yet move they had, slowly, inexorably, all the way from Independence, Missouri, seven hundred gruelling miles back east to this remote desert land crossing the Black

Rock Desert. Another month pushing relentlessly west, they'd see the purple rise of timber clad mountains topped in snowy white, the final barrier to reach fertile valleys on the far side. Struggling across this dangerous land seemed nearly a lifetime for many. For the foolish or unlucky, it would be the end of theirs. Those that made it would realize their dream where a man could put down roots, raise a family, break rich, virgin ground to grow abundant crops and raise fat cattle. That single dream drove them on.

Keen had made this same epic journey as scout, trail blazer and protector of wagon pioneers for nine previous springs. He knew that exact timing was vital for success and for life its very self. He had to cross half a continent at the slow pace of oxen or horses pulling fully loaded wagons, yet do so before the killing heat of summer in western deserts and before the first snows of fall fell, blocking the steep trail over the last mountains. His darkly tanned face and rangy build clothed in buckskins made him look like a man older than his relatively young thirty-one years. His penetrating eyes and face also held another secret rarely divulged to anyone. Will Keen carried the blood of a Paiute grandfather coursing through his veins, the very same Paiutes into whose land he was now leading the wagon train.

One hundred and seven men, women and children in those prairie schooners had put their lives, faith, trust and last dollar into Keen's promise to lead them across half a continent to the promised land over mountains far to the west. He was their leader, their guide, their Indian fighter, and the only law they'd know until claiming homesteads in Oregon Territory. The single crack of an ambush rifle or the hissing flight of a flint-tipped arrow could change all those cherished plans in an instant.

The arid lands the wagon train now entered was the domain of the Paiute people, still living wild and free as they always had. They were as hard and fierce as the land that spawned their ancestors thousands of years earlier. They bitterly resisted the intrusion of white men into their land, whether they came to dig for silver or gold, or moved through in long lines of wagons. Paiute warriors travelled in small bands using hit-and-run tactics, then disappeared back into their wilderness. The lone wagoneer who abandoned the safety of larger wagon trains to try some new trail or a supposed short cut, was quickly cut down to become only food for vultures. This was not the open grass prairies and broad river valleys back east where danger could be easily spotted still miles away. This twisted, broken land of endless box canyons and deep ravines easily hid attackers until the final moment before they bolted from cover on paint ponies yelling war cries.

Keen had to stay in the saddle, in the lead, every minute of the day, post guards every night and often stay awake supervising men who were farmers and merchants who never fired a weapon of any kind in their entire lives, let alone at another human being. It was a sudden transition some could never make. That meant Will had to make it for them. Looking ahead Will gauged what time he had left before a lowering sun ended another long day in the saddle. He needed time for a meeting with all drivers about the trail ahead.

Wrangel Foot in the lead wagon saw Keen riding in. Easing back on the reins of his four oxen team, he pulled to a stop. Standing in the box Foot raised his hand, signalling to the others behind him. 'How's it look up ahead, Will?' he called out.

'We're going into canyon country. The land closes in fast. I want all the wagon drivers together so I can talk to them.'

'That'll take some time, won't it? Shouldn't we use as much daylight as we can to keep on going?'

'No. Another few miles won't mean much this late in the day. Get your men together. We're going into dangerous country. I want everyone made aware of that and how to handle it.'

'All right,' Foot shrugged, easing down off the seat. 'Eustace, get up here and mind the team,' he yelled to his brother in the back of the wagon. 'They're so tired and thirsty, it won't take much to hold them.'

A smoky sagebrush fire barely lit the shadowed faces of drivers that evening standing in a circle with Will in the middle. Behind the drivers the women and children, bundled against the desert chill of evening, stood silently listening as he slowly walked the circle looking each driver in the face, emphasizing his remarks.

'By now you all know we're starting into Paiute country. I've seen enough sign to know they've passed through here not too long ago. They probably know we're coming in, too. Whether they mean trouble or not is up to them. What's ahead of us is largely canyon country. It's steep and chopped up with lots of side canyons and deep washes where it's easy for trouble to hide in. I want all you men to keep weapons, if you have any, up front where you can get at them fast if you need to. Once we start in I also want the wagons close together nose to tailgate, in line. There'll be no stopping to eat, drink or rest. Only a wagon breakdown would change that. If that does happen, we all stop together. No one gets left back even if they're in plain sight of the rest of the wagons. The Paiutes can over-run a lone wagon faster than I can say it. When we stop for the night I want all the horses tied on a picket line and a night guard watching them. Wrangel Foot will decide who takes turns on that. Your oxen should also be kept close. Any of them wander off during the night and you'll never see them again. They'll end up on a Paiute fire pit.'

'How much time do you think it will take for us to get through this country ahead?' one of the drivers called out.

'That depends on how long you can work your teams each day. There's very little water ahead. The only water you'll have for at least the next two weeks is what you can carry in your water barrels. When you're thirsty, save that drink for your animals instead. The Black Rock desert we came through was bad enough. Now we'll be into a high desert almost as bone dry. If your animals falter, you're in trouble. From here to the western mountain passes, water will be more valuable than gold. Remember that.'

'Do you believe we're still on time to cross over those mountains into Oregon?' Foot raised his hand.

'I'd say we're doing about right on time at least up to now. A lot can happen between here and that high country that no one has any control over. That includes me. If we're careful and don't have too many setbacks, we'll have a good chance to make it. Don't forget there's always a chance for early snow — that could change things, too.

'There's nothing I can do about the weather. We'll all have to keep at it each day, and see how many miles we can cover.'

'My horse team is getting pretty thin

and worn out without anything to eat up here but sage and bitter brush,' one of the wagon men complained.

'All I can tell you is if your animals are struggling, you might want to ask your woman and adult children if they can get out of the wagons and walk a while. It will lighten the load and make it easier on your animals. But just remember, anyone on foot has to stay close to the wagons. Don't drop back or stop even for a short rest. I'll be out front where I can't see or help you if you get into any kind of trouble. I'll suggest one other thing. If you see your animals are in trouble, think about unloading anything you don't absolutely have to have once you settle down in Oregon Territory.'

'Like what?' a driver questioned. 'Everything me and my wife own is in our wagon.'

'Like musical instruments, a piano, furniture, frying pans, extra trunk full of pots and pans you don't need. Anything that adds extra weight.'

'I'm not sure I can do that after we hauled our belongings all the way back from Missouri.' Another driver shook his head before Foot spoke up.

'You all better listen to what Will is saying. He's done this before with other folks and knows what he's talking about. We can all share our tools and labour once we settle in over the mountains. The only thing that counts now is getting there. If someone does break down so bad we can't fix it here on the trail, then they'll have to leave most of their things and double up in another family wagon. That makes it even harder on the animals. If you think your animals are in trouble, get rid of what you don't need now before it's too late!'

The first thin halo of grey invaded the blackness of eastern sky while Will and Wrangel stood sipping a cup of hot black coffee, next to a flickering fire. An oxen bellowed out behind sleeping wagons and a horse whinnied. Foot studied his scout's emotionless face a moment before speaking.

'I'd have to say none of us in this wagon train have ever been sorry we hired you to take us all the way to Oregon, Will. So far you've done everything you said you would. I want you to know I speak for all the others when I say how much we appreciate that. None of us knew what we were really getting into. I guess no one could unless they took it on themselves.'

Keen nodded at the wagon master before speaking. 'I was brought up to believe a man's word was his bond. I still do. I know all your people are counting on me, just like the other parties I've brought west over the years. That kind of responsibility helps my thinking stay pretty clear. I know a lot of lives are at stake.'

'So far, I'd say crossing the Black Rock desert was the toughest thing we've had to endure. You seemed to know that stretch of misery like the back of your hand. I'm real glad you did. We could have lost animals and people, too, out there without those springs you took us to.'

'I ought to know it. I was raised up in

11

those rocky hills on a little horse ranch on the far side of the Black Rock. My mother pretty much raised me by herself sometimes with the help of her brother.'

'You didn't have a father?'

'I did, but he only came back home long enough to put together another grub stake before leaving again, chasing gold fever. He always thought he'd strike it rich someplace around the desert mountains, if he could just find the right canyon. As far as we knew he never did. When he didn't return after another trip we didn't know if a diggings had caved in on him, if a band of renegade Indians had killed him, or if he just left the country for someplace else. Before all that the Paiutes use to water their horses at a spring behind our ranch house, when I was a kid.'

'The Paiutes!'

'Yes, that's right. When I was ten years old they taught me how to make small bows and arrows so we could hunt wood rats together. I learned how to live in desert country because of them early in life. Black Antelope, Small Eagle and One Eye were my friends.'

'Are those the same Paiutes you're so worried about now? You think they'd still be your friends, wouldn't they?'

'I really don't know. Maybe not. Your wagon train isn't the first settlers I've brought through their country. They probably know that, too.'

Foot rubbed the back of his neck thinking over the surprising revelations. He had another question for his scout. 'Here's something else I don't understand. We've pulled these wagons across half a continent and through other areas that were tribal ground without much trouble. Why are you so concerned now about this stretch of country we're in? Are the Paiutes any different?'

'In some ways they are. These people have always lived in this land where no others can, and that includes whites. They've learned how to survive and make the most out of very little. But now their water-holes are being poisoned by dead oxen and horses. The cavalry sometimes

13

rides up here raiding villages, and they kill not just men, but women and children, too. A few prospectors are beginning to come in looking for gold, digging in their sacred land, if they're not killed first. The Paiutes are a people who have lost nearly everything they ever had. All they have left is to fight for the only way of life they've ever known. Ask yourself this. What would you, me or any of your people in these wagons do if someone tried to run us out of our homes and off our land too?'

Foot stood struggling for an answer. He had none. Will broke the uncomfortable silence. 'Thanks for the coffee. I've got to saddle up Blue, and get going out front. Here comes tomorrow,' he nodded toward the growing rim of dawn. 'One other thing. If you see me today or any other day riding in fast firing my pistol, that means trouble is right behind me. Take action to pull the wagons to a stop. Order everyone to arm themselves. I hope that does not happen, but it's always best to have a plan if it does.'

The wagon master nodded with a parting thought. 'We'll talk again like this, Will. I can learn a lot from you about this harsh country and the people in it. Watch yourself out there today. I don't know what any of us would do without you.'

Keen kept the wagon train moving as steadily as possible all that next week, keeping to open flats and wide brushlands, away from the cover of surrounding hills and endless side canyons where trouble could lurk. The worn wagon-wheel ruts of previous springs' passage still marked the way in most places. Where wind and what little winter rainfall there was had washed away the trail, he had to rely on memory and the lie of the land. Yet even his sharp eyes did not see the distant image of a small party of Paiute braves shadowing him and the wagons from the cover of hills paralleling the trail.

Led by Black Antelope, the six braves not only had vengeance on their mind because another wagon train was invading their high, lonely domain, but the burning question of whether or not three white men who had come riding into their village stealing food and water at gunpoint, were hiding someplace in one of those wagons. When an old man in the village had tried to stop the three from taking two young girls, they'd shot him down. Black Antelope had trailed the three in this direction for three days until finding the line of wagons. If he had to attack to find and take those three, he was prepared to do so.

Driven as he was, Black Antelope could not help but notice the lone rider far ahead of the wagons, marking trail. Even at a distance he could see that rider was no white man. Instead he wore buckskin clothes, and his face was darker than the men at the reins in those wagons. He seemed to have no fear for his safety, his long rifle snug in a skin scabbard on the side of his horse. His manner and steady advance through the country alone demanded that Black Antelope learn who he was, and why he rode so boldly through a land that was not his. Near sundown after another long day leading the wagons, the Paiute leader decided it was time he get that answer face to face.

Keen rounded a bend in the trail where brushy hills pinched close together narrowing the trail. Suddenly he reined Blue to a halt, instantly pulling his six gun. Ahead of him not fifty feet away, a lone Indian warrior sat his horse, rifle in hand, staring hard at this strange man who always rode far ahead. For several tense seconds neither man spoke or made a move, each strangely fascinated with the look of the other. Black Antelope dared to urge his horse forward another few yards, his eyes boring into the buckskin-clad man. Will kept the pistol tight in his hand, nerves tingling, ready to use it. But something made him hold back, he wasn't sure why. Maybe it was a fleeting memory. He decided to take a chance to speak.

'If you understand my language — I am not here to fight. I want only to bring the wagons behind me through here and be gone. Do you know what I have said?' He held his breath waiting for any sign or reaction.

Black Antelope nodded slowly. Now he suddenly realized who this strange trail breaker was. 'Do you remember how to speak the tongue of a young boy?' He stunned Will with his demanding question.

'If you mean — the few words of Paiute I once knew, I might.' Will leaned closer trying desperately to recognize the dark lined face of his inquisitor.

'We called you — Running Boy.'

Will's face lit up in amazement. He remembered a name he hadn't heard in years, the same one his Paiute playmates once called him.

Holstering his pistol he edged Blue right up alongside the brave studying his face even closer. It was older, more scarred, worn by time and strife, but he began to recognize it. 'Black Antelope, is that — you?'

The Paiute nodded without smiling.

'I have watched you for three suns. I knew you were not a white man. Now I know who you are, but not why you bring wagons through our land.'

'They only want to pass through and will not stay. They go far away over the mountains where the sun sets.' He pointed west. 'They are farmers who plant seeds and grow crops. They fight no one.'

'You do that for them?'

The gravity of the question caught Will off guard. He could not let it pass without a truthful answer. A lie would only make more trouble. 'I would fight for them if I had no other choice. I am only here to take them far away to a new land.'

Black Antelope didn't question his statement, his eyes boring into his old boyhood friend for any sign of deceit. Finding none, he asked another question.

'Three white men came to our village while my braves and I were out hunting. They took all the food and water. They killed an old man who tried to stop them from taking two young girls. Their trail has led me close to here. Are those three hiding in your wagons?'

'They are not. I tell you the truth. I will swear it on my mother's grave.'

The dark-skinned man leaned back on his horse a moment longer, never taking his eyes off Keen. He believed what he said, and decided to continue. 'One of these men wears white hair. He does all the talking. Another has black hair, and black eyes too. The other one is young with a twisted face. He makes strange sounds, sometimes like a bird. I want these three. I will not turn back until I take them.'

'I have not seen any of these men you talk about. If I do and can find you, I will tell you where they are.'

Black Antelope nodded, looking Will up and down one final time. 'You have grown tall and strong, Running Boy. I knew it could be no other way. You have been gone many moons from this land. When you have taken these white eyes to that land over the mountains, come back here and live as you once did with us. Always remember you carry the blood of our people in your veins. This is the land you know best.'

'I will think on it, my old friend. I promise I will. Now will you let us pass?'

The brave nodded without uttering another word. Reining his horse around, Will watched him ride away. The chance meeting seemed so strange, so unpredictable after all these years, flooding back memories of his boyhood. He couldn't help but wonder if the gods of the ancient ones had directed it to happen, or if it was only blind chance. That question would never leave his mind for years to come.

2

Riding back towards the wagon train, Will pondered the information his old friend had given him. In place of his original worry that the Paiutes might attack the wagons, now a new threat loomed large: the three white men who had raided the Indian village. Were they somewhere nearby in this vast lonely land, as Black Antelope thought? If they were, something as easy to see as a line of twenty-three canvas-topped wagons moving slowly against the backdrop of the monotonous grey-brown of the high desert would make easy targets.

Keen suspected the three had likely been involved in a lot more than raiding the Paiute village and kidnapping two young girls. Men who would do that were vicious enough to try almost anything, regardless of how reckless or cruel. If they did find the wagons, he'd have to take on all three alone. The wagoneers were not stand-up face-to-face gunfighters. Before he reached the wagons he'd already decided it would be best to call a meeting of everyone and explain what they might be facing, and how he wanted them to react if it did happen.

'We may not see these three men and have nothing to worry about,' Will stood in front of the pioneers that evening, most in the company of their wives and children. 'But if they do happen to show up I do not want any of you to try and use weapons to stop them. That's my job. I don't want anyone else getting hurt because of it. The sooner we get through this country and farther west, the better our chances will be that it won't happen. Keep that in mind near the end of each day when you're tired and want to stop to make camp. We need to put as many miles behind us as possible. When we do we leave that kind of trouble behind too.'

A small current of whispered suspicion rippled through the uneasy crowd at the thought of more trouble. They were already stretched thin. Now just when they had news the Indians would let them pass, Will had to bring up a new threat of danger.

'You better be right about this, Keen,' one man shouted. 'Just how sure are you the Indians will let us pass? What good is their word?'

'I know them. I grew up with some of them. If they say so I believe they mean it.'

'If you're wrong about this we'll all be in for the fight of our lives, in this God-forsaken land!' A second doubter called out.

'Wait just a minute here!' Wrangel Foot walked out of the crowd to stand next to Will. 'Have all of you forgotten who got us this far? And have you forgotten who has kept us out of all kinds of trouble that we could have faced? You better think on that instead of doubting what Will says now. If he says the Indians will let us pass, I believe him. So should all of you. This new possible trouble with the men who raided their village is what we ought to be paying attention to now.'

'Remember this,' Will finished the meeting. 'You're not back in Missouri any more. Out here not every white man is a saint, and not every Indian is a killer, either. Everyone should get a good night's sleep, because we're starting out earlier in the morning. We've still got a lot of rough country to go through ahead of us, and both you and your animals are going to need every ounce of strength possible.' Keen's warning could not have proved truer. What little open ground they once had quickly faded into larger, yawning canyons, steep drop-offs and in some places sheer rock cliffs. Slippery down slopes became so dangerous that the animals had to be unharnessed, then roped to the rear of the wagons acting like a brake, with drivers on the reins walking alongside them to keep the heavy wagons from breaking loose and careening uncontrolled into the canyon bottoms, shattering into splinters and maiming or killing the drivers. The slow, arduous, time-consuming work required hour after hour of back-breaking physical effort to move all twenty-three wagons ahead up one canyon and down another hair-raising drop-off. On their worst days the wagon train barely made ten miles, falling behind the schedule Will had set for them to reach the final mountain barrier, still out of sight far ahead.

After each day of sweat-filled misery, most men and their families were so tired they didn't even bother building cooking fires, eating cold meals before falling exhausted into bed. The strain and struggle caused tempers to flare as some accused others of not doing their share of the work. Friends became bitter enemies, families pitted against each other to the point where both Will and Foot had to mediate endless battles and disagreements at the end of each day. Everyone was on edge except Will, who would not let himself fall into the quagmire of defeat.

His saving grace came each morning

when he rode out ahead of the wagons puzzling out the route for that day, away from all the resentment and petty arguments that grew into major battles for some. The endless task of finding the best way through canyon country day after day almost made him forget about the three men who had raided the village now nearly two weeks ago. He would be reminded of it just when he thought that threat was left somewhere back behind them in the hard-fought miles and maze of twisted canyons they'd fought their way through.

★　★　★

Burl Peet, K.C. Coons and young Dylan Trapp sat on their horses on the rim of a limestone drop-off watching the distant blink of white-topped wagons slowly moving, five miles away.

'Would you look at that.' Peet pushed out his chin, eyes narrowing as he studied the surprising discovery. 'Just when I thought we were about to starve to death, the grocery store shows up way out here in the middle of no place to save us. How about that, Coons?' He turned to his partner.

'I'd say after that Indian slop we've been trying to eat, some white man's food ought to go down real easy. All we have to do is ride out there and take it.'

'What about you, Dylan? Like what you see, boy?' Peet questioned.

Trapp threw back his head barking out a loud, drawn-out wolf howl.

'I'll take that as a yes, you half wit.' Burl shook his head in dismay. 'Sometimes I wonder why I ever took this bird brain in with us.' He turned to Coons.

'Because he's a dead shot with either a six gun or rifle, even if he is a little cracked in the head. You saw how fast he put that Indian down, didn't you?'

Burl nodded, hating to admit Coons was right. 'Let's get down there to those wagons and get real neighbourly. I can almost smell a good meal from here. And we might find something else worth taking while we're at it.'

Keen caught the distant movement of riders on the move out of the corner of his eye, pulling Blue to a sudden stop. Three men atop those horses could only mean one thing. His worst fears were being realized. The trouble he'd hoped to avoid was closing in on the wagons at a fast gallop. He wheeled Blue around kicking away flat out to intercept them.

'Hey, who's that!' Coons shouted, pointing at Keen galloping towards them whipping his horse, closing fast.

'I don't know, but he don't exactly look friendly, riding like that!' Burl shouted. 'Let's pull up and take him at close range if he means to make trouble.'

The three riders slowed to a halt watching the buckskin clad man loom larger until he reached them, pulling to a dusty stop, sliding his rifle out of its scabbard up across his lap quick to get at.

'What's your rush, mister?' Burl challenged first. 'A man could get himself shot, riding in like you just did without a call.'

Coons and Trapp didn't say a word, each eyeing Keen, his weapons and buckskin clothes suspiciously as he answered.

'Where do you three think you're going?' Will never took his eyes off the trio and their gun hands, reining Blue between the trio and the wagons still far out.

'Who's asking?' Peet shot back, the clear edge of sarcasm in his voice.

'I am. I'm the scout for those wagons out there. All of them are my responsibility, if that's where you think you were going.'

'Well yeah, we're hungry and fresh out of food. Have been for days. We figured those God-fearing sod busters don't want to see a man starve to death out here, do they?'

'It's not up to them. It's up to me. And I say they need what food they have for themselves. I don't want them sharing it with anyone else.'

'How would you know what they want?' Peet kept at it. 'There has to be enough food in all those wagons to feed us and ten more like us. I say we let them decide if they can spare just one plate of vitals or not.'

'No, they're not. I decide that for them and I've already told you they won't. You'll have to find help someplace else to feed yourself. It won't be here.'

'What are you talking about, skin man?' Coons finally spoke up, irritated at the back and forth of words. 'Who do you think you are, trying to order us around!' His hand naturally moved down towards his six gun, but Keen instantly swung his rifle barrel directly on him only six feet away. It had a sudden, sobering effect.

'You touch that hog leg an' you'll never clear the holster,' Will warned in a low, steady voice, eyes locked on Coons. 'You three best clear out and get moving while you can. If I see you again, there won't be any talking. I'm telling you to stay away from my wagons. You'd better listen.'

'That's not very neighbourly of you,

mister,' Peet spoke up again. 'Three against one is pretty short odds to be bossing men around you don't know.'

'Not really. I know you and I know your type. Have you been to an Indian village lately, and do you know where those young girls are you took?'

Peet glanced at his partners with a quick look of surprise, but Keen wasn't finished yet.

'And don't think the odds worry me. They don't. I'll get two of you before I fall, and I'll be sure to make you're first,' he motioned toward Peet. 'You think that's worth trying to get a free meal?'

Burl stared back with his mouth half open but without a smart mouth answer this time. It took him a moment before he could try.

'We'll meet you again.' He eyed the buckskin-clad man in cold contempt. 'But like you said, there won't be any talking to it. Let's go, you two!' He pulled his horse around, starting away. Dylan Trapp, the last in line, looked over his shoulder with a lunatic smile on his face and waved goodbye, whistling like a bird. Will still sat in the saddle, never taking his eyes off the trio until they were only dots lost in surrounding hills. He'd had a good look at what he was facing. This time he had come out on top, but there would be a next time, there was no doubt about that. He wondered if he'd still have an edge then.

★   ★   ★

After pulling his lead wagon to a stop, Wrangel Foot stood from the seat watching the distant knot of riders break up, wondering what the strange meeting was all about. He had an odd feeling that it wasn't good news. Watching Will ride in he shouted a question.

'Who was that, out there, Will?'

'Three men we didn't want to see. It looks like the ones who raided the Paiute village. They're going to be our problem now. It's just a matter of time before they come back. When they do, my guess is it will be at night. I'll have to remind everyone tonight not to try and go up against them. None of you would stand a chance against a bunch like that. They're loaded and looking for more trouble. I'll want two men to stand night watch as long as we're in this canyon country. If I'm asleep and they show up, they'll have to wake me and fast. I probably won't be getting much sleep anyway now. Sooner or later I'll have to deal with them.'

'But you don't stand a chance by yourself against three men. I know at least some of our people will stand with you, and that includes me.'

'Have you ever pulled a six gun, rifle or shotgun on another man?'

'Well — no, but I think maybe I could — if I had to.'

'And while you're thinking about it it's already too late. Same goes for your people. Everyone will have to stay out of it and let me handle it. When they do come in I want you to get all the women and children back in the wagons. I don't want anyone else getting hurt. You understand me?'

Foot nodded, his brow already furrowed in worry, wondering how much time they all had before the confrontation that Will was so sure of would take place. The next three days as the wagons continued fighting their way through steep canyon country, the image of the three riders was always in view, paralleling them far out. Each night when they pulled to a stop, tension-driven fear hung over the pioneer camp like a dark cloud. The men said little, their eyes always searching out into the dark, while the women fixed quick meals so everyone could eat early and return to the safety of their wagons.

Keen had watched the distant riders too, reducing his usual several miles ahead of the wagons to just a few hundred yards, so he could ride back quickly if needed. After sundown on the evening of the fourth day a sudden cold wind came whipping across the sagelands, sending tumbleweeds scurrying past the wagons and out into the night. Will stood by a struggling fire, drinking a cup of hot coffee. Foot and several other men turned their backs to the gusts, pulling their jacket collars up higher.

'What kind of country is this, anyway?' one driver questioned. 'We sweat all day like hogs in the heat, then nearly freeze to death at night. I hope once we get over the mountains we leave this country as far behind as a bad memory.'

'It is different over there,' Keen acknowledged, 'Mostly sunny summers, fall and winter rains. Just what you folks need for growing crops and raising stock. The high desert here mostly grows hard people and bitter memories, but it wasn't always that way.'

'When wasn't it?' another driver questioned.

'Before whites started coming west the Paiutes were always nomadic people. They travelled through the land following the seasons, moving from these highlands in winter down to the flats, then back

36

up again in spring. They followed and hunted animals like deer and antelope. It was never an easy life, but they knew how to survive in it. They are people of the land that spawned them.'

'I believe I'll turn in for the night,' another man said. 'See you all in the morning.'

'Me too,' a second agreed. 'I know Will wants to get an early start.'

'What about you, you going to get yourself some shut-eye?' Foot asked his trail scout.

'Not yet. You go ahead. I'm going to stay up a little longer. I want to give Blue some oats, and try to get this fire a little higher.'

'All right. See you tomorrow, Will. Good night.'

'Night, Wrangel. Tell your wife thanks for the coffee. This was the perfect night for it.'

'I will.' The wagon master disappeared into the dark towards his wagon.

Will knelt by the fire feeding sputtering flames a handful of fresh sage stalks.

Standing, he turned his back to new flames warming himself, staring out into the night. Those three men were out there someplace watching, he was certain of that. He could feel unseen eyes on the silent line of wagons and his meagre fire. And he knew why they had not come in yet, letting the days pass. They wanted the fear of a confrontation to sink deep into the minds of all the pioneers, who would wonder and worry why they had not come in. That kind of fear could paralyse decent folks into inaction.

'Hello, the wagons!' A voice suddenly shattered the night wind. 'We're coming in. Don't do anything you'll regret!'

Will stepped away from the fire out to the edge of the light, trying not to silhouette himself, his hand moving down to touch the cold walnut grips on his six gun. Slowly, one by one, the image of three men on foot leading their horses came out of the dark, their faces made grotesque by the shadowed play of firelight.

'We figured it was time to drop in and say how do,' Burl Peet came to a stop, looking around to see if Keen had any help from wagoneers.

'You should have saved yourself the trouble. I told you once before you're not wanted here,' Keen warned. 'You don't listen very well.'

Peet pushed Coons and Trapp away from him on both sides so they weren't standing close together, making easy targets. 'We figured you had time to regret being so unneighbourly. Now we've come to get us that food we want. We ain't asking for it anymore either. If you're smart, you won't try to get in the way and get yourself shot. Know what I mean? What's it going to be, skin man?'

Will took a few steps back to get a better angle on the three with one last order. 'Get back on your horses while you can. This isn't a Paiute village with women and children which you can walk into and take what you want.'

Peet glanced at his pals wondering how the buckskin man could know about that, but not for long. 'Have it your way.' Peet's voice was suddenly low, menacing. 'We'll take what we want even if it's over your dead body. Take'm boys!'

Trapp was fastest, his six gun clearing the holster the same instant Will's did. Both men fired simultaneously, the kid driven back by the impact of Will's bullet, crumpling to the ground kicking and screaming. Will dived for the ground as Peet and Coons cleared their pistols, firing wildly at his rolling shadow behind the campfire, before he came up on his knees, pistol flaming. Coons took his second and third bullets and went down in a heap, as Peet backpedalled fast, emptying his pistol. Will felt the white-hot whiplash of a bullet cutting into his flesh, driving his leg out from under him. A second bullet caught him high in the shoulder, as Peet ran back for his horse. Will fired his last shots at his vanishing figure, hearing Peet cry out in pain before the sound of horses' hoofs pounded away into the night, ending the sudden gunfight.

Will lay on the ground face up, trying to catch his breath through a web of spreading pain. The sound of running feet and shouting voices came near until the faces of several men hovered over him, everyone trying to talk at once.

'Stop yelling and get me some bandages and hot water!' Wrangel Foot ordered, trying to quell the mayhem as he knelt next to Will. 'And take a look at those other two over there on the ground too!'

The last thing Will remembered before blacking out was many hands slowly lifting him, and being carried away with the acrid smell of gun smoke still hanging on the night air.

He woke squinting against the bright glare of sunlight through the canvas wagon top above him. Confused for a moment, trying to remember what had happened and where he was, he started to sit up. The wall of pain that instantly shot through him brought everything back into intense focus. He collapsed back into thick covers, gritting his teeth. The pretty young face of Foot's teenage daughter Sarah suddenly appeared leaning over him mopping his sweat-drenched face with a wet cloth.

'Try not to move around. You'll only start bleeding again. Mom, Dad,' she called over her shoulder. 'Mr Keen is awake. Come quick.'

Wrangel kneeled next to Will, the concern on his face obvious even through his thick dark beard. 'I'm real glad you're awake,' he rested a hand on Will's arm. 'You lost some blood. We finally stopped it, but you're as full of holes as a prairie dog town. You won't be in the saddle for a good long time like this, Will.'

'What about — the other three?' Keen questioned.

'You killed two of them. Looks like one got away. We found a blood trail until it petered out. Don't know if he went off and died, or if he's still running.'

'Why — aren't we moving?'

'Moving where? We don't know the trail. We can't start again until you're well enough to ride, and that's going to be a while. All we'd do on our own is wander around and get lost. I told the rest of the men to give their animals a rest until I talked to you.'

'You can't do that. We have to reach the mountains before the weather changes and maybe the first snow falls. If this wagon train sits out here waiting for me to get back in the saddle, it'll be too late. All of you will have to spend the winter on this side of the mountains, and even have to build shelters or cabins waiting until spring comes. You can't make it through winter in these wagons. Neither can your animals. You have to keep moving. There's no choice in it.'

Wrangel straightened up, staring at his wife Dolores and daughter. He had to make a decision and fast. The wrong one could doom the entire wagon train and everyone in it. He took in a deep breath, trying to rub the worry out of the back of his neck. He had one hundred and twenty-three souls that could live or die because of what he decided now. His mind raced as he stood staring down at Will a moment longer. 'All right then. You called it. We'll start out in the morning. The only way I can do that is to have you up front in the seat whether you're in pain or not. I'll prop you up between me and Dolores. I just hope you don't bleed to death trying it.'

3

With the dawn could be seen the figures of men on the move, hitching up oxen and horses to wagons, their wives putting out cooking fires, packing up utensils and bedding. Wrangle Foot and Dolores gingerly helped Will to his feet, then struggled to get him up front on to the spring seat on their wagon. Dolores folded several blankets for padding to help cushion Will's pain even just sitting. Sarah retrieved his jacket placing it over his shoulders against the morning chill. Wrangel looked over at Will with deep concern.

'You ready to try this?'

'I am,' he nodded. 'Let's get to it.'

Wrangel stood for a moment leaning out so other wagoneers in the line behind could see him. With a wave of his hand he shouted. 'Let's roll 'em!'

Twenty-three Conestogas rumbled

forwards, wheels turning, their animals straining at the traces, drivers cracking leather woven whips over their backs. One by one they began pulling away from the overnight campsite until the last one passed, leaving deep wheel tracks in flinty ground, while off to one side two fresh mounds of dirt rose over unmarked graves. K.C. Coons and Dylan Trapp had met eternity in the high sagelands beyond the blinding glare of the deserts. No one would mourn their passing or know their fate except Peet, Keen and the pioneers. The final barrier of western mountains lay someplace still far ahead — but one other wounded man was also struggling to reach them, although no one in those wagons knew it.

★   ★   ★

Far ahead of the wagon train, Burl Peet rode slumped low in the saddle, eyes half closed trying to fight off the excruciating pain of not one, but two bullet wounds. His knee-high boots had a perfectly round .45 calibre bullet hole half way up his leg, and a vicious gash across the left side of his face was wrapped in a bloody bandana. Even as Keen went down in the gunfight back at camp, he'd gotten off two shots that had hit home. Peet's throbbing head felt as if it would explode, and his leg was nearly useless, but he was still alive. The thought of revenge would keep him alive, even though he was half out of his mind with pain.

Peet and his two pals had made a living preying on small parties of men struggling to reach either the gold fields of the Sierra Nevada mountains or the fertile valleys farther north in Oregon Territory. Desperate dreamers who had taken the chance to come west in only two or three wagons were also easy pickings for the trio. They robbed the men of money, sometimes even took their horses, leaving them afoot, and cleaned out the wagons of anything valuable including the life savings of the families in them. Most of these innocent victims either had no weapons to defend themselves, or if they did, were too afraid to actually use them against the three men who made it clear they'd kill anyone who tried to stop them. The pioneers in Wrangel's wagon train might have fallen to the same fate except for Will Keen's presence leading them.

Peet's base of operation was over the high mountains ahead on the eastern slope of the Cascade Range in the isolated town of Cedarville. The one thing that would keep him going was the chance to someday find Will Keen again and kill him for what he'd done. He lifted his head trying to focus on the fuzzy image of monotonous, rolling sagelands ahead. He closed his eyes clinging desperately to the saddle. Only death would stop him from reaching Cedarville and the help he needed to survive.

★ ★ ★

Keen sat propped up between Wrangel and his wife as the wagon rattled forwards, jostling from side to side and causing him to grunt with pain while trying to pick out the trail ahead. More than once because he couldn't be out front on Blue, he'd chosen the wrong way, forcing all the wagons to stop and laboriously turn around so as to retrace their steps. The following three days proved to be no different. At the end of the fourth day, Will lay in the back of the wagon propped up on pillows, spooning hot soup into his mouth, realizing they could not continue this way. Sarah sat close changing his bandages with her mother and father nearby finishing their soup. The young teenage girl studied the worry on Will's face. At first she said nothing, but by the time her mother gathered up the bowls, she couldn't hold back any longer.

'Is the pain still pretty bad, Mr Keen?' she asked, causing Wrangel and Dolores to look up. Will glanced at both of them, worried about what he'd been thinking, knowing now he had to say it out loud. The look on his face made it clear he was struggling.

'What is it, Will? Speak up. If we can help you know we will,' Wrangel was quick to offer.

Keen took in a long, slow breath. There was no easy way to say it. He hated having to put more worry on these decent, good-hearted people, but felt now he had no other choice.

'At the rate we've been moving each day and having to turn around trying to find the trail, there's no way we'll reach the mountains before winter sets in. We're making less than ten miles some days. I thought maybe I could make it work being here in the wagon, but I can't. Without being on Blue, well out front where I can see the lie of the land, or sometimes even old wheel tracks, before the wagons reach me, this isn't working. If I could just get back in the saddle again, we'd be all right. I know everyone is doing their best, but I hate to have to admit this isn't going to work.'

'Now wait a minute, Will.' Foot put a hand on his shoulder. 'Everyone in this wagon train owes their life to you and what you've done. They won't quit because we miss a trail. I haven't heard one single complaint from anyone, and that's the truth. We'll figure out something else if you're so sure we have to. Maybe one of the other drivers could ride point and do the job?'

'I don't think that would work either. Each man has to take care of their own family and wagon team. Besides, none of them has ever broken trail before. They'd get lost or take the wrong way just as quick. You'd all end up having to turn around several times each day like we've been doing. If I could handle your team, I'd let you take point, but I can't. I need someone who can follow my directions and get back to me fast so I can explain what to look for up ahead.'

The four sat silently for several

seconds before Sarah suddenly spoke up. 'I can ride, and you can tell me which way to go if I lose the trail.' She shocked all three of them, but her father most of all. He had a quick response: 'Absolutely not!' His face turned red with anger. 'Don't you even think of something like that. It makes no sense, and you know it, Sarah. You're a girl — or I mean a young lady. You're no trail scout, for God's sake!'

'I am not a girl. I'm already eighteen, and I've been riding horses since I was six years old. You married Mom when she was just seventeen. Do you think she wasn't old enough to make a decision like that?'

'Now wait a minute — I didn't mean — I'm not saying you're not grown up, but this is too dangerous. Mother, will you try to talk some sense into her. She won't listen to me!'

'Sarah, all your father is trying to say is that there isn't another man in this entire wagon train that can do what Will does. It isn't about you riding a horse.

We've already had a gunfight and killing right here in camp, and even Indians trailing us. What do you think would happen to you out there alone if they showed up again? We'd never forgive ourselves if something bad took place. I understand you wanting to help, but we've all come too far to take a chance like that.'

Sarah grasped her mother's hand before looking at her father and Will. 'Yes, I do understand what you're saying. There could be some danger, but I also heard what Will said, and so did you. We won't make it over the mountains unless we can move faster and farther each day. I don't have to ride five miles ahead like Will did. I can stay only a mile or so out front, just far enough so the wagons don't get trapped again and have to all turn around like we've been doing. If I see trouble coming I can ride back here fast. It can work, Mother. I know it can. Please let me try, for all of us.'

Dolores sat dumbfounded at her

daughter's argument. It actually made some sense, and she couldn't deny they were already falling far behind the original schedule. She looked at Wrangel, who didn't know whether to be mad or proud at Sarah's insistence to help. Both turned to Will, praying he could talk Sarah out of it.

'Your mom and dad are naturally worried and scared about this, and with good reason. This isn't a horseback ride back home in the pasture on your folks' farm.'

'See,' Wrangel joined in, nodding with relief. 'Listen to Will. He knows how dangerous this is. Go ahead, tell her Will.'

'I do, but I have to say Sarah is young and strong. She could stay in the saddle as long as any man. And if she did stay close to us in the lead wagon, she could get back here fast where we can cover her. Her idea just might work. I can tell her what to look for and how to pick up the old trail. If she loses it she can ride back and I'll help her out.'

Wrangel's face dropped. He couldn't believe what he was hearing. He had thought Will would talk Sarah out of her wild idea, but instead he was practically encouraging it. Dolores was equally shocked, and quickly said so.

'Will, you can't be serious. Sarah may be good with horses, but not doing what you did. She's no gunfighter, and those Indians I mentioned could come back too, couldn't they?'

'They might, and I know it sounds risky, but it might not be as bad as you and Wrangel think. The three who tried to rob the wagons are dead. The Paiutes won't harm anyone here. I know them. I've talked with their leader, Black Antelope. I'm certain about this, and just to be sure I'd give Sarah this to wear.'

Will lifted a leather thong necklace hidden in his buckskin shirt over his head, motioning Sarah to lean closer so he could place it around her neck. The necklace was strung with brightly coloured stone beads. In its centre, three small silver coins with holes drilled through their centre finished the strange-looking amulet. Wrangel and Dolores looked at each other, wondering what this odd jewellery could possibly mean. Will saw the question in their eyes, too.

'No Paiute will harm Sarah while she wears this. These beads were given to me by a medicine man and they show he was my friend. The coins were my mother's. Her spirit lives on in them, which is why I always keep them close to my heart. If you two decide to let Sarah try this, these things will protect her from harm. That choice is up to you. I cannot make it for you. I do think we need to try something to reach the mountains in time to cross over. If Sarah is careful and listens to me, I can show her how.'

The pretty young woman looked to her mother and father. Tears began moistening Dolores's cheeks. Wrangel's head dropped, and he sighed out loud, struggling to come up with his answer.

Dolores reached out grasping Sarah's hand, waiting for her husband to speak.

'I guess, maybe — we can try this once. I just hope to God I don't regret going along with it. If something happened to her, I'd hold you responsible, Will. I have to tell you that man to man, even though I call you a friend.'

'I understand. I'll do everything I can to be sure it works and keep Sarah safe at the same time. I can promise you that.'

Keen spent a good part of that morning carefully explaining to Sarah where the old trail should be, how to recognize it, and what to look for if she couldn't find worn wagon tracks. He taught her to look ahead as far as possible, trying to see the lie of the land, and picking out the easiest route so wagons wouldn't get stuck in a dead end or soft ground, having to turn around as they'd done before. He cautioned her to remember not only to watch ahead, but all around as they moved forwards, always on the alert for any sign of trouble, whatever it might be. Even if she had no need to ride back to the lead wagon he wanted her to check back at least once an hour so they could discuss what she saw and if it would be familiar to Will too, so he could help her puzzle out the way ahead. The last thing he suggested was that she ride Blue, telling her the horse could recognize the old trail from memory often times as well as he could. When he finished she had a question for him.

'Should I take one of your guns, Will?'

'Not my pistol, but my rifle is in the saddle scabbard. If you wanted to use it to signal me for some reason you could. Have you ever fired a rifle before?'

'No, I haven't.' She shook her head, her long auburn hair tumbling to her shoulders.

'Here, I'll show you how. Put the gun to your shoulder like this, pull the hammer back until you hear it click, and keep it snug against your shoulder so the kick doesn't hurt you. Remember, only use it if you have to, and get back here fast.'

Finishing her lessons and saddling Blue, Sarah rode up alongside the canvas-topped wagon looking at her mom and dad. 'You've got one tall horse, Will!' She flashed them a nervous smile.

'Yes he is, but he'll outrun anything else on four feet if you ask him to. You know what we talked about. Keep your mind in the middle and you'll be all right. I'll be watching out for you, too. If you hear me fire a shot that means I want you to get back here fast.'

'I will.' She gave a quick wave, kicking Blue away ahead of the wagons.

'I never thought I'd see the day I'd go along with something like this,' Wrangel mumbled, his brow furrowed in worry. 'I'm not going to rest easy until this day is done and she's back here with us.'

Dolores stayed tight-lipped, while Will tried to ignore the comment. He'd supported Sarah's idea, and now he had no choice but to stand by it, trying to keep her from harm no matter what it was. Out here in the high desert, that could be a long list of things very few people ever thought of ahead of time. A broken wagon axle, waterhole gone dry, animals too sick, weak or underfed to continue pulling wagons, all spelled serious trouble.

Sarah's heart beat faster under Will's buckskin jacket, as the wagons dwindled away behind her. She was on her own, doing what her mother and father never thought she could, reciting Will's orders over and over to herself. Always, as the wagon train moved slowly ahead that first day, they were surrounded by sagebrush hills fronting lofty limestone cliffs. Twice before noon, she'd ridden back to ask Will questions. Each time he patiently explained away the problem. Early that afternoon she rode back again alarmed, telling him she thought she'd seen distant riders paralleling them.

'They could be Paiute braves keeping an eye on us. We're getting close to the limit of their territory. They might only want to be sure we leave. If you see them coming closer, get back here fast and I'll handle it. You're doing good. We're making better time, I can see that already. Maybe in another week or so I might even be able to get back in the saddle. I do miss not being out there, and worry about you too.'

'I'll get better every day with all you've taught me. I might not want to just sit in a wagon all day long after this. I know it's a little dangerous, but it's exciting to be out front trying to lead the wagons. If you do try to ride, I'd still like to be in the saddle too.'

'That would still be up to your mother and father. For now keep your eyes open. You will get better at it, but don't get too comfortable. That's when trouble can show up when you least expect it.'

Will watched her spur Blue away at a steady gallop, and thought what a great homesteader she would be, helping her mother and father start a new life in Oregon Territory. A new life. The thought made him pause for a moment. What about his own life? He'd been leading wagon trains like this one for nearly ten years across half a continent, yet he really had no place to put down roots like all these pioneers did. He'd fulfilled the dream of hundreds, or maybe even thousands of people wanting to start a new life in a new land, but in all that time he'd never thought much about what he might do, if and when he decided to settle down someplace. He'd stayed briefly in scattered cow towns, army outposts and wagon camps where pioneers gathered to sign contracts before their long trek west, but he had no place to call home. Maybe, he thought, it was his Paiute blood that always kept him moving. They were nomadic people. So was he. It had taken disabling gunshot wounds to make him sit still and think about these things for the first time. They were sudden, sobering thoughts that made him uncomfortable.

He was still a young man at

thirty-three years old, and the only thought of what home meant was the old stone-walled ranch house where his mother had raised him all those years ago on the edge of the Black Rock desert. He wondered if it was even still there, or if it had been brought down by the ravages of time. The desert was a cruel taskmaster, taking back all things left abandoned by man. Did the canyon behind the old house still have that bubbling spring, he wondered, gushing ice-cold water to the surface, giving life to the scattering of white-barked Quaking Aspen trees surrounding it.

'I think I see a patch of green up ahead!' Wrangel's shout broke Will's day dreaming.

'That could be Volcano Springs,' Keen answered, squinting at the image ahead. 'If it is, we're on the right trail, thanks to your daughter. I'll know for sure when we get closer. The Paiute people have always used it.'

Volcano Springs stuck out in the drab landscape of endless sagebrush like a bright green beacon. Fed by underground springs through rocky fissures, it was a sudden oasis to previous wagon trains, and certainly to this one, too. The pioneers needed a short rest, and so did their weary animals. Now they could water them and themselves, and top off nearly empty water barrels for the next long leg of the journey, where no water would be found. The springs got their name from the rocky, volcano-shaped vent from which life-giving liquid steadily bubbled up. Wrangel Foot pulled his lead wagon to a stop alongside the copse of trees, followed by the other drivers. Women and children rushed from the wagons and knelt around the spring, drinking icy cold water before filling pails and buckets to the top. Sarah rode up alongside her father's wagon with a smile on her sun-burnt face.

'This is a wonderful surprise, isn't it, Dad? Will, you knew it was here, didn't you?'

'I did, but the fact you led the wagons to it shows me you're getting good at riding point. You ought to be proud of yourself. I'm a little proud of you too.'

'What about you, Dad? Do you think I'm doing a good job, like Will said?'

Wrangel's face flashed a small grimace. He didn't want to encourage Sarah further, but he had to admit she'd done much better than he'd ever expected. 'I guess you are, but I'd still feel a whole lot better if you were back in the wagon with me and your mother, and Will was back riding out front.'

She smiled back. She still had unspoken plans to ride point even after Will got back in the saddle, but for now she'd keep that little secret to herself and not upset her father even more.

Evening descended on the circle of wagons around the spring, lit by many flickering campfires. The heat of day had long since disappeared as a cool evening chill came over the camp. Someplace far off, a coyote howled. Moments later another answered with his evening song. Will raised his head from watching the dancing flames, listening to the eerie song of the desert. Wrangel and several other men had helped lift him from the wagon down around the firepit. One of the drivers spoke up.

'Are those wolves, out there?'

'No, coyotes,' Will answered. 'Paiute people say they are the smartest spirits of all. They know how to steal whatever they want, then vanish like smoke, and they can change into anything else they want to be.'

'That's just Indian mumbo jumbo, isn't it, Will?' Wrangel scoffed.

'No, they don't think so. They've lived in this land with them long before any whites ever came through here. They must have a good reason to believe it.'

Dolores changed the subject. She knew Will wouldn't mock the Indians and thought it best to break in. 'Let me change your bandages while I still have some firelight left to see what I'm doing,' she quickly suggested.

'I'll get the bandages, Mom.' Sarah got to her feet, walked to the wagon and climbed inside.

While waiting for her to return, several drivers came out of the dark up to Wrangel's campfire. 'Evening Wrangel, Missus Foot and Will. We aren't interrupting anything are we?'

'Not at all, Horace. What's on your mind?' Foot questioned.

'Me and several other drivers was wondering how close we are to reaching the mountains? We've gone through a lot of our supplies, and need to figure out how much longer we have to stretch them out?'

'Will is the man to ask about that. What about it?' Foot turned to the scout, all eyes following him.

'If we can keep moving like we're doing now with Sarah out front, I'd say we'll reach the high country in about another two weeks, or maybe a bit longer depending on how things go here with all the wagons. Does that help you out?'

'Two weeks?' one man lamented. 'That's cutting it pretty close for some of these folks. Are there any towns or military posts before that?'

'No, not until we get up into the Cascade Range. There's one small town there called Cedarville. You might buy some food and supplies there, but the cost will be high because they have to freight everything in from the valleys farther west. Those valleys are where all you folks want to put down homesteads.'

The drivers looked at each other with sullen faces. This wasn't the kind of news they'd hoped for. Will saw the anxiety too. He decided to try to take some of the sting out of his remarks. 'If I can get back in the saddle again, I might be able to cut some time off that two weeks. Wrangel, his wife and Sarah have been taking pretty good care of me. I can even move around a bit for the first time. Soon as I can ride, I will.'

'We're all glad you're feeling better Will, but we sure hoped we'd be leaving this desert behind sooner than that. Fact is some of our folks are just about out of everything they need. My woman even had to start making soup for dinner because we're trying to keep what little food we have left for what's ahead. She don't even throw away the bones any more. Our oxen are in just about the same shape. Some of these other wagons just might not make it another two weeks or more?'

'All I can tell you is what I said before, to lighten your wagons again if you have to. Get rid of everything you don't absolutely have to have. Ask your woman and older children if they can walk a while each day. That will help your animals, too. Remember if your animals fail, all the food or supplies in the world won't be worth two bits. If things are getting this bad maybe Wrangel might want to call a meeting of everyone to discuss food sharing for those who need it.'

'I can do that,' Foot spoke right up. 'In fact you men pass it down the line to meet me right here in the morning, and we'll go over all of this. Good idea, Will. Thanks for suggesting it.'

4

The morning sun barely peeked its first fiery rim over rocky buttes, when a big circle of drivers and their families gathered around Foot's campsite, some women and children wrapped in blankets against the nighttime cold. Will sat in the wagon seat next to Dolores and Sarah, as Wrangel called the meeting to order and began talking. He had a lot to talk about, and much to convince his charges into doing. Those that could spare a bit of extra food had to make it available to families who were running short. He began, fiery in oratory, ordering the crowd that it was their mission demanded by God, to help the less fortunate. Wrangel knew that some families, and maybe even a majority, might instead want to keep every single bit of supplies they had for themselves for what still lay ahead so they didn't run short too.

When he finished half an hour later, sweat ran down his face red with emotion. For several seconds men and women stood transfixed by his demands to help until a few heads nodded and one by one people began speaking up pledging they would give up what they could. Even Will had to comment on his success.

'I've never seen Wrangel like that. He really means what he says and knows how to make others believe it.'

'Yes,' Dolores replied a smile on her lips. 'That's why they chose him to lead this wagon train. My husband is a man of God driven for everyone to honour the Good Book. He's always let it guide him throughout his life. You believe in the bible too, don't you Will?'

Keen had never been asked a question like that before and it took him back for a moment. He didn't want to hurt Dolores' feelings, and he didn't want to lie about it either. Yet he had to tell the truth. His hesitation brought the same question back a second time.

'You do, don't you? I'd hate to think any different. You're too decent a man to be otherwise.'

Will's slow half smile seemed odd to her but it was his way of trying to calm both.

'Dolores, you know I've got Paiute blood in me, don't you?'

'Yes, I do, but I don't hold that against you for any reason. You don't look or act like a Paiute either.'

'I know that. But I was raised up with those people and their beliefs, and I learned at a young age to believe in them, too. They believe in many gods and not just one. What we just saw Wrangel do was talk about one of those gods. That's fine with me, but it doesn't mean other gods should be mocked, or those who believe in them be looked down on. Do you understand what I'm trying to say? I hope you do, because you and your family have been so good to me. I know you are godly people too.'

Dolores stared back stunned by Will's

bold pronouncement. She didn't want to question his beliefs, but had clearly taken too much for granted. And she didn't want Will to think she thought any less of him because of what he'd said. Before she could make amends, Sarah put a hand on Will's shoulder getting his attention.

'Mom didn't mean anything by it, Will. She's a good Christian woman brought up with her beliefs in the bible, just like you were with your friends. You both believe in something deeply, and that's all that really matters to any of us, isn't it?'

Keen stared hard at the beautiful young woman whose words were so adult and understanding. 'That's right, Sarah. I wish I could have said that as well as you just did.'

Wrangel ordered everyone to their wagons to bring what they could spare back to him, forming a line. Sarah and her mother got down from their wagon and took the food and supplies, putting them in the back of the wagon to be distributed to whoever ran short and needed help. It took another hour to assemble all the goods before the wagons could hook up their animals and begin to move out again.

'You should have been a preacher, Wrangel,' Keen commented after the wagon leader climbed into the seat next to him handling the reins.

Foot's grey whiskered face cracked in a quick smile. 'You don't know how close you are to the truth. I was studying to be just that when I first met Dolores. That changed everything for me. But I still feel the 'calling' from time to time.'

'Yes, I saw it at work just now,' Will admitted as the wagon lurched forwards, following Sarah already riding ahead in the lead. 'You've still got the fire for it. We may need that again, but next time not for food.'

If Foot wondered what Will meant by that remark, he didn't ask. For some strange reason he felt it best not to. It almost had an ominous tone to it.

★ ★ ★

The beckoning heights of the Cascade Mountains still lay too far ahead for the wagon train to see, but one other rider had finally reached their pine-studded slopes. Burl Peet's bloody wounds plagued him constantly with endless misery. Only his stubborn resolve to live long enough to wreak vengeance on Will Keen kept him in the saddle each day. Reaching the first icy creek dancing down from above, he pulled to a halt, painfully lowered himself out of the saddle, and dragging his wounded leg behind him, collapsed next to the rushing little waterway. Plunging his throbbing head into the water he drank until he came up coughing and spitting, fighting for air. But the sudden shock of the chilling water seemed to clear his head a moment. Reaching up, he unwrapped the bloody rag covering his head wound, and slowly washed it, trying to clean the ghastly gash on the side of his face. When he peered down into the little pool he barely recognized

75

himself, his face red, swollen, out of shape.

Peet rolled over on to his back. He had to get his boot off to soak the leg wound in cold water too. He struggled groaning, the boot tight over the blood-soaked sock and pant leg. It wouldn't budge. Gasping for breath he fished out his belt knife, and slowly edging the blade into the boot top, cut his way down inch by inch until he reached the ankle. With a shout of pain he forced the boot off and submerged his leg in the water. His mind raced as he lay there, trying to remember how many more days he needed to reach Cedarville. Was it seven, ten, more? He couldn't seem to concentrate through the fog of endless pain, loudly cussing himself for not being able to.

Slowly sitting upright, he rewrapped the rag around his head, carefully pulled on what was left of his boot, and struggling to his feet, staggered to his horse still drinking a few feet away. Pulling himself up into the saddle again, Burl

Peet did at least remember one thing. He vowed to make it back to Cedarville, even if he rode into the mountain town dead and stiff in the saddle. Somehow, some way, he had to stay alive to face Will Keen again to even the score with his flaming six gun.

What Peet couldn't see through his misery were the first fingers of grey-bellied clouds slowly drifting in, high over the peaks still miles ahead — the first sign that an early fall was coming fast to the Cascade Range. Those too slow to make it over the mountains before snow fell would suffer because of it, whether it was Burl Peet or the wagon men still many miles away out in the high desert.

* * *

High up in those mountains Oren Heck stepped outside a run-down shack up-canyon from Cedarville, pulling his jacket collar higher around his neck, eyeing the dark clouds drifting by overhead.

'Hey, Zack,' he yelled back inside the cabin. 'We got enough firewood for tonight? Looks like we're gonna' need it if this weather keeps going downhill.'

Zack Minx came to the door and stepped outside. His narrow, hawk-like face and small, darting eyes give him the appearance of a predator, a description as good as any that summed up his entire adult life. Both he and Heck had helped Burl Peet on various occasions in robberies and beatings of small groups of prospectors trying to cross the mountains heading into the Sierra Nevada goldfields to the south, and also small wagon outfits passing close to, or through Cedarville. Peet sometimes even stayed in their cabin avoiding men in town for a few days whom they'd mugged at night as they left the saloons staggering drunk. Heck turned his heavily whiskered face to his shackmate with a question.

'How long's Peet been gone, you remember?'

'Ahhh . . . I'd say nearly a month. He lit out of here with two other pals of his.

That sound about right?'

'If it is, he might be coyote bait by now. Him and those other boys were looking to take down some sod busters, if they could find any. They should have been back by now, especially with this weather coming on.'

'Yeah, if we get early snow, there won't be anyone trying to make it over the top, and we won't have no chance to make some more cash. We might even have to scare up some kind of work in town.'

Heck turned with a sudden look of disgust on his face. 'A job, are you crazy? No one's going to hire us except maybe sweeping floors and emptying spittoons, down at the Mountain House. I ain't gonna' do that no matter how hungry I get. I'd eat a skunk first!'

Minx stared back with a blank expression on his face. 'Maybe we ought to try and ride out a-ways and see if we can find Peet? He's always got some cash on him.'

'He could be anywhere, especially if

he went all the way down to the desert like he said. That's way too far to go now. I say let's wait him out for another week or so. If he don't show by then, maybe we'll have to do some 'work' on our own.'

Minx scratched his head, thinking over the suggestion. He wasn't sure he liked the idea that much, so he made one of his own. 'For now, why don't we just head down to the Mountain House, and see if we can get a free drink? Cold as it's getting I could use something to warm me up.'

'I might go for that, but first you'd better be sure we have enough wood for tonight. This cold is coming on, I can feel it in my bones.'

★   ★   ★

The wagon train continued plodding steadily west over the next week, with Wrangel and his wife handing out food and supplies that others had donated to help out the needy. Those supplies dwindled faster than either thought they would. Slowly, imperceptibly, the desert began to change each day from surrounding deep canyons and towering cliffs, to rolling, open sagelands with long flats in between. Sarah, still riding out front, reached a low rise and reined Blue to a stop. Far ahead on the horizon, the jagged silhouette of mountains marched across the skyline. Above the peaks dark clouds hid their tops. Her heart skipped a beat at the stunning sight, and she immediately pulled Blue around and galloped fast back towards the wagons, shouting and waving her arms as she closed in.

'Will, Will, I see mountains up ahead!'

Keen told Wrangel to pull to a stop as Sarah rode in alongside the wagon, wide-eyed with the discovery, a big smile on her excited face.

'Are you sure that's what you saw, Sarah?' Keen questioned.

'I am, Will. They're still far ahead, but they're across the whole skyline as far as I could see. There are clouds over most of them, but they must be the Cascades you're always talking about. They're too big to be anything else!'

Keen looked over at Wrangel then back to Sarah. 'I've got to try and get in the saddle and take a look for myself. That's the only way I can be sure. Help me down. You too, Sarah.'

'I'm going with you. We can ride double. Besides, you might need me for support,' Sarah insisted.

'You'll do no such thing, young lady. You stay right here and let Will try to get out there on his own, if he thinks he can!'

'No Daddy, I'm going. I didn't make all this up. It is mountains and he might need my help. He hasn't been in the saddle for weeks. I want to show him what I saw.'

Wrangel started to insist, but Dolores put a hand on his arm and he turned to her.

'Let her go, Wrangel. Let her show Will and all of us what she found. It means nothing more than that. Now please help Will down and up in that saddle. Let's see if we're finally getting close. That's more important than anything else right now.'

Wrangel stared back at his wife a moment, unable to find the right words. She rarely contradicted him. When she did, it made him stop and listen. Slowly he stood from the seat offering a hand to Will. 'All right. If Dolores thinks it's OK, I'll allow it this time. Come on, Will, can you stand?'

Keen grimaced as he settled into the saddle, while Sarah climbed on behind him, wrapping both arms around his waist. He urged Blue forwards, first at a walk, but able to take the pain in his leg, he urged him ahead at a faster gallop, heading for the ridge a quarter mile ahead. Reaching it he pulled Blue to a stop, studying the line of dark blue mountains far ahead. For a moment he did not speak. When he did, he validated all Sarah had said.

'You're right. That is the Cascades.

They're still a long ways away, but now we have something everyone can see to drive for. It's time for me to get back in the saddle too. I think I've had enough healing. I'll have to get used to riding again, especially as we get closer.'

'Then I'm riding with you!' she blurted out.

'You can't do that, Sarah. You've done a good job, now it's time to get back in the wagon with your mother and father. I'll be all right out here again.'

'That's not what I want. I want to be out front too, not sitting in that wagon day after day. I like riding on point, on the move, seeing everything that lies ahead. I won't get in your way, I promise you. I'll ride one of Daddy's horses. You can have Blue all to yourself, not ride double like this.'

'Sarah, I wish you'd think a little bit more about such a wild idea. As we get closer to those mountains, everything could change. It could get a lot more dangerous, and I can't just look out for you, but have to look out for everyone in those wagons behind us, too. Remember those three men at the gunfight that night in camp?'

'I do, but I've been riding point since you were wounded, and I've done a good job. You said so yourself. I wasn't threatened in any way, was I?'

Will could see arguing with her wasn't working. He shook his head still feeling her arms around his waist, her warm breath on the back of his neck as she spoke. He didn't want to admit to himself that he liked that feeling, even if she didn't realize it. It was something he hadn't felt in a long time, and this was no time or place for it. He wouldn't let himself think there ever could be a time either.

'Talk to your folks, Sarah. They're not going to let you do something like that. I know your dad won't allow it. Leave me out of it. It's no place for me to be any part of, anyway.'

'I will talk to them. I'm not a child who can be scolded because she decides to do something on her own.

I'll tell them that I want to ride point too, whether they like it or not.'

Will didn't answer this time. The entire conversation had grown far too personal. He knew from long experience leading pioneers west to avoid any kind of personal involvement with his charges. His only job was to bring the men, women and children who had put their well being and very lives in his hands safely through to the land of their dreams, and nothing more. This sudden interaction with Sarah Foot had come upon him so unexpectedly he hadn't realized how far things had come. He realized he had to avoid becoming part of her argument with her parents, for his own good. The ride back to the wagons was made in complete silence.

Will determined to spend as little time as possible with Wrangel and his family outside the wagon, and those dinners he took with them were largely done with as little discussion of anything but the trail ahead as possible. The unspoken tension between those brief discussions was so thick you could cut it with a knife. Sometimes while eating Will would glance up to see Sarah always looking back at him. He knew she had been arguing with her mother and father about joining him on point. He quickly looked away to avoid any conversation about her demand.

Four days later one afternoon as Will sat in the saddle stopping to choose the trail ahead, he heard the sound of horses' hoofs coming up fast behind him. Twisting in the saddle he saw Sarah, mounted on one of her father's horses, closing in. Pulling to a stop she wore a smile of victory on her face — but one that Will did not match.

'I told you I'd be back out here, didn't I, Will? I had to convince Mom and Dad I was right, and they finally listened to me.'

Keen's face was an expressionless mask, but the thoughts behind it were many and came fast. A degree of anger drove those thoughts, too. When he spoke it was with one penetrating remark: 'You convinced everyone but me, Sarah. Why didn't you think of that?'

The self-assured smile suddenly faded from her face and she struggled to answer him.

'I thought you wanted me out here helping you. You know I can do it.'

'It isn't a matter of what you thought or wanted. With you out here I have to worry not only about the wagons and everyone else in them, but you too. That's what you should have been thinking about, and not just yourself. You see those mountains up ahead?'

She nodded but did not speak. 'When we reach them it's going to take all my time to get these wagons up and over the top, without trying to keep an eye on you. That's another thing you should have thought about. That high country can be just as bad as the deserts we're crossing, maybe even worse. We've left the Paiutes behind, but what's up there can be another kind of trouble. I don't want to face it worrying about you, because I will.'

His comments cut into Sarah's resolve so completely she had to question what she'd done. After winning her freedom, he was dashing all her hopes. She turned away so he couldn't see the hurt in her eyes as tears began running down her face.

'All right, Will. If you don't want me with you I'll go back. I thought you'd like having me here. I can see now you don't.'

She started to pull her horse around, but Will reached over and grabbed the reins, stopping her. 'Listen to me and try to understand something, Sarah. Maybe in another time and place all this would be different. I'd want you with me. But not now, with what I'll have to do when we reach those mountains. You have to understand that.'

She didn't answer, but reined the horse around and started back to the wagons, with tears still streaking her face.

* * *

That night up in the Cascades the first silent curtains of snow fell. By dawn the land and everything in it was covered in a carpet of glistening white. Half way up into those mountains a horse and rider plodded ahead, both covered in snow. Head down, eyes nearly closed, Burl Peet clung desperately to the saddle horn with hands nearly frozen stiff. When he raised his head squinting at the world around him, he wasn't sure if he was on the trail to Cedarville or not. In his dim awareness, half alive, all he could do was pray the horse knew where he was going. Peet hunched lower in the saddle wondering if hell could be any worse than this. Late that day when cloudy skies hid the setting sun, he pulled the animal to a stop and dragged himself from the saddle to crawl up under the branches of a small pine tree. He didn't build a fire because his hands couldn't work to strike the matches stowed in his jacket pocket. The horse stood head down, still saddled, shivering in the increasing cold of the growing darkness.

Dawn came. A weak sun peeked through holes in clouds, waking the delirious man. He lay there a long time wondering if he could get up into the saddle. Slowly, painfully, he rolled on to his knees, grabbed the saddle stirrups with one hand and pulled himself upright, and with a shout of pain struggled into the saddle. If God wouldn't help him, Satan did.

★   ★   ★

Later that afternoon Peet suddenly smelled something besides the stench from his bloody wounds. It was the drifting smoke of fires. He raised his head to see snowy rooftops through scattered timber close ahead. At last, against all odds, Burl Peet had made his miraculous ride all the way back to Cedarville, more dead than alive, but alive nonetheless.

5

'Get that fire going while I cut off his frozen clothes!' Oren Heck ordered his pal, half dragging Peet over to a bunk where he collapsed in a heap.

'Look at his face! It's all swollen out of shape,' Minx winced at the grisly sight. 'His leg is shot up too. If he can talk, ask him what happened, and where the other two that were with him are?'

Heck ignored the question, stripping off bloody clothes while Peet groaned out loud every time he pulled off another piece. Before covering him up with a blanket, he leaned closer eyeing the wounds. 'The bullet wound in his leg went clear through. Don't look like there's any broken bone.'

'What about his head?' Minx questioned. 'It looks like it's about to explode!'

'The bullet grazed his head but didn't go in. If it had, he wouldn't have made it back here, that's for sure. Get me some rags so I can try to clean him up a little bit.'

'There ain't no doctor around here and there's no way he'd make the ride over the mountains to Happy Valley,' Minx said.

'I'll do what I can, but if he's gonna' die I can't stop it. He'll have to make it on his own. I know one other thing for sure. No Indians did this to him. He'd never rode out of the desert if they'd caught him. It had to be someone else.'

★ ★ ★

The strength in Will's legs slowly returned, even though the pain of his wounds still kept him grimacing when he moved too fast. The silent tension between him and Sarah remained evident through the brief time he spent with the family eating dinner each night. He always turned any conversation to the trail ahead, and the crucial timing needed to get over the mountains, which were now close enough for their snowy heights to be seen by everyone in the wagon train.

Over the next eight days Will began angling the Conestogas north-west, aiming for the rough wagon road that started where the alkali flats of the desert met the first abrupt up-thrust of foothills. Just before they reached them, he asked Wrangel Foot to call the drivers and their families to another evening meeting. That night a crackling camp fire sent golden cinders into the night sky as Will walked in a slow circle explaining to the crowd what to expect in the days ahead.

'All of you can see we're getting close to starting up into the Cascades. The first part won't be too much of a problem because there's only a scattering of snow down low. But as we climb higher, that's going to change. It's obvious to me an early fall has already started in the mountains. Last time I brought settlers through here what little snow we had was only in the tops, and even that was what was left over from the previous winter. This time it's different, and it means the snow is going to make more work for all of you and me. Normally I'd wait a few days before starting up, to give your animals a rest, but this early weather now makes that impossible. As soon as we reach the foothills we're going to start right up. Be prepared for it.'

'Didn't you say there was some kind of town up there?' A driver raised his hand.

'Yes, Cedarville. But if you have to buy food or supplies, the cost might be too high for most of you. They make their money from wagon trains after they've crossed the desert and are low on goods. You won't find any buys up there. You'd best use the extra food and supplies all of you donated that Wrangel and Dolores have in their wagon. If you have to cut back on meals, now is the time to start. It's another three weeks until we top out and start down the other side. You'll have to make what you have last the best you can. One good thing is once we do get up into the mountains you won't have to worry about water for either you or your animals, and there's meadow grass for them to graze on. They'll need it. Break out your warm clothes, too. Once we start up it's going to stay cold both day and night.'

Three days later the line of wagons rattled to a stop as Will came riding back holding up his hand. He pulled to a stop at Wrangel's lead wagon, prompting the grey bearded leader to stand up from his seat.

'Looks like we're here at last Will,' he called out with a weary smile.

'We are, but before we go any further I want both of us to go down the line and pick out three or four of the strongest wagon teams.'

'What for?' Wrangel cocked his head, and Sarah and her mother sitting next to him wondered why, too.

'I want them up front to open up the road once we get into mud or snow. It will make it easier on the rest of the line that are not as strong. They'll all get tired soon enough. I don't want that to happen down here. I only hope the grass and water farther up will give all the animals what they lost after crossing the desert.'

'All right, let's go take a look at them.'

The two men picked out four wagons and had them pull to the head of the line while Will talked briefly to each driver explaining they had to keep their eyes on him for signals whether to slow down, speed up in the bad spots, or come to a fast stop. He pulled on a heavy buckskin jacket and gloves before taking one last look down the line. With a quick wave of his hand, all the wagons lurched forwards, and began the long climb up into the dangerous Cascades.

* * *

High up in those mountains Burl Peet leaned on the front door of his pals' cabin, with a blanket wrapped over his shoulders and a cup of last night's oily coffee in his hands. In the weeks since

Heck and Minx had found him and taken him in, he'd slowly begun to heal from his wounds, which would have killed a lesser man. He stared out into a world of snowy white, an icy wind cutting his face, to which he seemed oblivious. Vengeance had stoked his miraculous recovery, while the name 'Will Keen' ran endlessly through his mind day and night. Like a nightmare without end, he vowed that the only way to stop it was to kill the man with that name. But slowly, day by day, he was getting stronger. When he could stand alone and pull a six-gun again, he'd know he was ready.

Peet also knew that the wagon train with Keen as their scout stood a good chance of eventually coming through Cedarville, but not when. However, there was another possibility that Keen could take a different route over the mountains, one that branched off the main trail before it reached town. If the wagons took that road he'd never get his chance to even the score.

'Burl, get back inside and close that door,' Heck called out. 'You're letting all the heat out.'

Heck's demand interrupted Peet's day dreaming, and he drained his cup and stepped back inside the cabin, up to the pot-bellied stove in the middle of the one-room shack.

'How're ya feeling, Burl?' Minx eyed him.

'Better. But I'm still not good enough yet to use a six-gun the way I should. It's coming along though. All I need is a little more time, that's all.'

'Time for what?' Zack asked.

'Time to get well enough to ride out and kill that wagon scout that did this to me. There's a good chance he might even come through town. If he does I want you two backing me up. I'll finish with him what he started out in the desert.'

Heck glanced at Minx before speaking up. 'Didn't you say he took down Trapp and Coons and damn near killed you too?'

99

'What if I did?'

'Because if he's that good I'm not sure you can count on me to go up against him. I'm not looking to start pushing up daisies anytime soon.'

'Yeah, me neither,' Zack intoned. 'Trapp might have been touched in the head, but he was a pretty fair hand with a six-gun. If he couldn't out-pull this wagon man, I know I sure can't either.'

Peet's face turned red with sudden anger. His lips quivered in reply. 'You two like the food and liquor I've been buying you since I got back?' He didn't wait for an answer. 'If you do, both of you better hitch up your belt and get some backbone, because when the time comes, whenever that is, you're gonna be there with me, or you can go back to nearly starving to death drinking pine tea!'

The Mountain House saloon was nearly empty later that week when its owner Rex Buckner came out from behind the bar and walked to the front door. Opening it he stood looking outside. A flurry of snowflakes were silently falling, coating the muddy street for a second time that day. 'It's going to be an early winter for sure,' he said as much to himself as the men at the bar. Business had been slower than expected all that summer, and now the prospect of winter so soon offered an even more dismal outlook. The only bit of real excitement had been Burl Peet riding back into town more dead than alive from out of the desert. Everyone knew Peet lived on the edge and crossed over it more than once. Local muggings and robberies in town made him the chief suspect. He'd said nothing to anyone about what had happened to him, and no one with any brain was about to ask. His bullet wounds answered a lot more about that than he ever would.

His pals Heck and Minx had taken him in, and that was the last anyone had seen of him in weeks. A few locals noted there was no fresh grave dug in the weedy cemetery back of town, so they figured he must be alive still. But the dreary days of a fast-moving winter were about to change in Cedarville, and change fast. Will Keen and the twenty-three wagons were halfway up the mountain, struggling slowly but steadily higher. The town was about to have visitors when they least expected it, and their arrival could result in an explosive confrontation of men not afraid to pull six-guns with the intent to kill to settle personal scores. Burl Peet had plenty of reason to settle his.

★　★　★

'Use your whips!' Keen shouted, riding down the line of labouring, canvas-topped wagons and animals. 'It's mixed mud and snow ahead. Don't let your teams slow or stop. You have to keep going through it!'

Drivers' whips whistled and cracked over the shaggy backs of their teams as wheels spun and oxen and horses strained against their leather traces. Will pulled Blue around riding back up to

Wrangel's lead wagon, using his short quirt to whip his horses ahead through deep slush, while Sarah and her mother hung on to the rocking wagon seat. Once Wrangel's wagon cleared the dangerous sinkhole, Will turned back to the next wagon in line, helping it through. One by one he steered each wagon in line through the same spot until all were in the clear.

By late that afternoon, dead tired drivers and their teams made early camp in a large snow meadow. The abundance of downed timber surrounding the big flat fed a huge bonfire that evening, its flames crackling higher than the wagons, with most of the pioneer families gathering there to warm themselves and ask questions of Keen and Foot.

'Are we close to Cedarville?' one man questioned while stamping his feet trying to keep them warm.

'We're just over half way there,' Keen answered. 'If we can keep up this pace we'll get there, but with more snow we have to pull through up higher.'

'I don't think my horses can take another week of this,' another driver shook his head in dismay. 'They're about worn out even now.'

'They'll have to. We can't stop and we can't turn back!' Wrangel's stern voice scolded the man. 'Might be we can ease the pace a little if Will thinks it's needed. We'll make it all right if we just use our heads and don't start thinking we won't. Don't let fear creep into your thinking, none of you.'

Keen continued: 'All of you remember this is some of the hardest part of the climbing. Once we reach Cedarville, we'll be nearly at the top. Keep that in mind. We're getting closer each day, and once we reach town we can take a short break if any of you folks want to rest a day or two or buy supplies. Three days out of there we'll top out over the Cascades and start down the other side. Everything will be easier on you and your animals when that happens. You've all come a long ways and done a good job of it. Don't weaken now when you're so close to having what you want. I'm proud of each and every one of you. I want all of you to know that.'

Wrangel beamed at Will's words of encouragement, and decided not to add to it. Dolores and Sarah were standing behind him and looked at each other, smiling. Will knew how to buck people up when they needed it most. It was a tactic nearly as important as the skills they'd learned after these many weeks on the trail. When the meeting broke up for the night and people began heading back to their wagons, Will stood by the fire alone thinking of the days ahead, until suddenly he became aware that someone was standing quietly close behind him. He turned to see Sarah.

'You surprised me,' he said, a flicker of a smile playing across her pretty face in the pulsing firelight. 'You'd better get back to your wagon. Your mother and father will be wondering where you are.'

'I'll only be here a minute. I want to talk to you, Will.'

'About what?'

'I want to know why you're staying away from us lately. The only time I see you is when you come to dinner, and you don't stay a minute after that either.'

'Because this is some of the toughest part of the entire trip to Oregon. Crossing over these mountains, especially now, with early snow, it's as hard on everyone as it was coming across the desert. I have to stay out front every day and help anyone who gets in trouble. You can understand that, can't you Sarah?'

'No, I can't. You've been trying to stay away from us since you made me go back and ride in the wagon. That's what I can understand. Am I right, Will?'

He stared back at her, even more uncomfortable with being confronted so abruptly. He knew he could not let himself get personally involved with her. It would be so easy to say yes. He did think about her every day but not now, not here, not under these conditions. He struggled to try and answer in some way that made sense.

'Sarah — I've got twenty-three wagons and the people in them to worry about each and every day. If I let myself worry about just one person, even you, I wouldn't be able to do what I have to. Everyone else would suffer because of it. I can't let that happen. These people have trusted me with their lives. What I might want or think about is not important. I can't let myself forget that, not even for one minute.'

'And you say that's the only reason you've stayed away?' Before he could answer she was at him again. 'I don't believe you, Will. Not one word of it. I think you're actually afraid to get close to me.'

'That's the only reason I'm going to admit to you. I'm thirty-one years old. I have no idea what I'm going to do after this wagon train reaches Oregon. You're nineteen. Can you understand what that means?'

'Before we reach Oregon, I'll have another birthday. I'll be twenty. I'm not a child, Will, so don't try to treat me like one. I know what I want, and who I want. Do I have to shame myself to tell you who that is?'

'No, please don't. Try to remember I still have a wagon train to get over these mountains, and as long as I do, that's what I have to concentrate on.'

She suddenly stepped close, trapping Will's face in both hands and quickly kissing him lightly on the lips, before turning away and running for her wagon, leaving him standing there looking after her, with even more trouble to worry about.

The wagons fought higher over the next six days until Keen topped a ridge near high noon and pulled Blue to a stop. Ahead, uphill through scattered timber, snowy rooftops with smoking chimneys could be seen. At last, Cedarville was finally in sight. He pulled Blue around, waving his arm in a circle for the wagons to come up.

⋆   ⋆   ⋆

Zack Minx walked out of Dawson's Dry Goods store in town with a sack of food Peet had sent him there for. As he stepped outside he quickly noticed several people pointing excitedly at the road leading into town. Following their gaze he saw a rider coming into view leading a growing line of canvas-topped wagons behind him up the snowy street. The man was dressed in a heavy buckskin jacket, pants and knee-high moccasin boots. His wide-brimmed hat was pulled low over his face, and he wore a red bandana across his nose against the icy wind. Minx's jaw dropped first in amazement, then fear. Was this the wagon scout Burl Peet had raved about killing, who had shot down Coons, Trapp, and him too? There was only one way to find out, and fast. He turned and started up the street, first at a fast walk, then breaking into a slipping, sliding run trying to keep his feet under him.

Minx ran all the way up the hill towards their shack, arriving out of breath, eyes bulging. As he neared the run-down structure he heard the sudden crack of pistol shots out at the back. Reaching the building he edged around to the back, not knowing what to expect until he turned the corner. Leaning against the wall trying to catch his breath he saw Peet standing a few yards away with his back to him, pulling his pistol and shooting at a tree stump twenty feet away. The .45 boomed twice more before Peet holstered the gun and turned to see Minx standing there wide-eyed.

'What are you so red faced about? You look like you saw a ghost.'

'Maybe I just did. There's a whole line of wagons coming into town right now with a rider leading them.'

Peet's reaction was instant. He stepped up and grabbed Minx by the jacket collar, pulling him so close he could feel his disgusting breath on his face. 'Are you sure?'

'Hell yes, I'm sure. I just seen 'em!'

'What did he look like? Tell me exactly what you saw!'

'Well — he looked sort of tall, wore

all buckskin clothes and boots, but had a bandana over his nose so I couldn't see much of his face. He rode a big grey mottled horse that almost looked sorta blue.'

Peet loosened his grip and stepped back, his eyes narrowing in thoughts of vengeance at the description. He'd prayed for months after nearly being killed that some day he'd get the chance to kill the man who had done that to him. He never thought that prayer would be answered so soon, with Will Keen actually delivering himself right into town. A wicked smile slowly came over his face. Pulling his revolver he began filling all six chambers with fresh cartridges. When he had finished, he looked up at Minx.

'You go get Heck. We're going to town. I want to see him for myself just to be sure. If you're right about this, he'll never leave Cedarville, unless it's in a pine box under a frozen grave!'

'Now wait a minute Burl, just hold on here. You already said he took down all three of you out there in the desert, didn't you? Me and Heck ain't no stand-up face-to-face gunfighters. We wouldn't stand a chance against anyone that good. We already told you if you want to ambush him that's something we might do, but not this. We'd be the ones filling those graves, not the buckskin man!'

'Listen to me, you little weasel. You better understand this right now. I want to see his face when my bullets cut into him, not shoot some town drunk from a dark alley like you and Heck do. Both of you better get that through your thick heads and get some backbone real quick, because all three of us are going into town!'

Store owners and their customers poured out on to the wooden sidewalk talking excitedly, some pointing and waving as wagon after wagon rolled down the street with Keen leading them. At the far end of town he had the wagons pull to a stop side by side, while their weary passengers climbed out to explore the town and enjoy the first civilization they'd seen in months. Most wanted to buy badly needed supplies they could afford, while Will gathered Wrangel and the drivers together with a suggestion.

'All your animals can use a good feed. Last time I was through here Lester Hays owned the livery stable in town. If you want to pool your money, I'd suggest you buy enough for your animals from him. He can even deliver it.'

Most of the men agreed, letting Will lead them back down the main street, while the women and children thronged both sides of the street, going in and out of the stores, thrilled to be able to buy at least some food and supplies they'd run short of after the desert crossing. The sudden influx of people and business had store owners smiling and cajoling their new-found customers after what had been a summer of little business. The mood was even carried out on to the street, with wide-eyed children pressing their faces to store windows, pointing and talking excitedly.

Sarah and her mother, arm in arm, came out of a store featuring gaily coloured bolts of cloth and other fabric goods, even a few dresses and pairs of shoes from back east. Dolores had bought several yards of calico cloth, which she carried wrapped in a package in her arms. But as they left the store they literally bumped into three men who had spent most of the night drinking at the Mountain House saloon. All three were well lubricated, though still able to stand.

'Well, look 'e here what we got!' One man nicknamed 'Goat' Kerr held both arms open, trying to encircle the two women. 'It's a pair of them nice wagon women just come into town.' He reeled on his feet, smiling stupidly.

'Yeah,' his whiskey-breath pal Pat Simms leaned closer. 'And I'll bet they'd just love to see the sights of Cedarville, after being out on that sagebrush sea for so long. They might even like to have a good dance or two. Wouldn't you, ladies?'

'Why don't we just squire them right back to the Mountain House, and tell ol' Buckner to break out a fresh bottle.' The third drinker, Mickey Gall, grabbed for Sarah who instantly lashed out, slapping him hard across his face, sending spittle flying from his lips.

'Why, you little spitfire!' Gall shouted, 'I like a woman with spunk. You'll do just fine once I tame you down!' He grabbed her with both hands while she fought back.

There wasn't a word of warning, only the sudden figure of a man coming up fast behind the three drinkers. Keen reached out, spinning Gall around with a thudding right into his jaw, sending him sprawling backwards into a horse trough with a resounding splash. Goat and Simms turned wide-eyed, staggering back from the intruder, as Gall's hand went down fumbling for his pistol. Will grabbed his gun arm with one hand and slammed him up against a store front wall, pulling his long-bladed hunting knife and pressing it hard against Gall's whiskered throat.

'You lift that six-gun, and I'm the last thing you'll ever see!' His voice was a low, sinister promise.

Gall's eyes bulged in fear at the cold steel pressing against his throat, and slowly lifted both hands in submission. 'You got me — don't cut me, mister — please don't,' he pleaded, his pals backing up into the knot of people who had gathered to watch the confrontation. Will reached down and pulled Gall's revolver from its holster, handing it to Sarah.

'You know how to unload this?' he asked.

She nodded. 'You showed me how, remember?' She opened the loading gate and turned the cylinders, dumping all six bullets on to the ground, then handed the weapon back to Keen, who shoved it back into Gall's holster with a warning.

'If I see you or your pals again anywhere near these ladies, or any other woman in this wagon train, you'll wish you'd kept your face in a bottle. You understand me?'

Gall nodded fast, still red-faced with fear, and backed away into the crowd, joining his other two friends, all three then quickly disappearing up the street.

'What's going on here, what happened?' Wrangel pushed his way through the throng. 'Is everyone all right?'

Dolores fell into his arms, shaken, explaining the terrifying encounter and how Will had stepped in to stop it. He looked over at Keen with a nod of appreciation. 'I don't know what we'd do without you, Will.'

'You'd do just fine, Wrangel, I know you would.' Will slid the big blade back into its scabbard, while Sarah stood staring at this man she was silently falling more deeply in love with, but who continued to keep his distance from her.

6

Burl Peet and his reluctant pals walked down Main Street just as the confrontation between Will Keen and the three whiskey-soaked boozers was breaking up. Peet suddenly held out his arm, stopping Heck and Minx, when they were close enough to see clearly the buckskin scout talking to Foot and his wife and daughter.

'Is that him, like I said?' Minx whispered, shrinking back and eyeing Peet for his reaction. Peet's intense stare answered the question without him uttering a word. He pulled the two men away so they wouldn't be seen, walking them back into the scattering group of onlookers.

'Yeah, that's him. That's a face I'll never forget. He won't forget mine, either, when I call him out' Peet's voice was a whispered threat of death.

'You ain't gonna do that right now, are you, Burl?' Heck questioned, praying at the same time the answer would be no.

'Not just yet. When the time is right we'll take him down. These wagons won't be leaving here for a while. We'll get our chance. I've got an idea, and if it works we might even get us some help, too.'

'*We'll* take him?' Minx's eyes widened. 'I thought you wanted to face him man to man? Me and Heck are only here for back-up in case you need us.'

'You two are going to be up front with me, like it or not. I expect both of you to do your part, not try to crawfish out of it when the gun play starts. I'm not going to tell you again to stand up like a man. You better be ready.'

The Mountain House saloon had its usual crowd of customers that evening, with most of the talk about the wagon train parked at the edge of town. Rex Buckner worked the bar, busy pouring drinks and talking with customers. One man at the bar called out as he filled another stubby glass with amber-coloured liquid:

'Hey Rex, you must be making a small fortune with all these pioneers coming into town, huh?'

'Not a dime. They're all bible thumpers. None of them believes in drinking alcohol. I don't expect them to start either.'

Burl Peet saw the chance he'd been waiting for, and spoke up first. 'They're not all God-fearing sod busters.' He turned at the end of the bar, facing the room full of men. 'Not by a long shot, they ain't. One of them is a half breed cold-blooded killer, and now that he's here where us civilized people live, he ought to pay for what he's done!'

The room suddenly went quiet as everyone eyed Peet, wondering what he was talking about. Buckner came down the bar until he faced him with a look of suspicion. Peet and his two pals didn't exactly have the reputation of being the most honest and trustworthy threesome in town. Everyone knew they often stepped outside the law, although they were rarely caught red-handed.

'What are you talking about? Do you even know yourself, or are you just trying to stir up some trouble?' Rex challenged.

'I'm talking about what happened to me and some friends east of here out in the desert over a month ago.'

'And what exactly was that?'

'I'll tell you what. Me and Dylan Trapp and K.C. Coons were out prospecting near the Black Rock desert, when Paiutes attacked us. We had to ride fast for our lives and leave our camp and supplies. We had no food or water for over a week when we ran into this wagon train here in town, and Will Keen. Instead of helping us like any civilized man would do, he told us to get out. When we tried to reason with him, he drew down on us and killed both Trapp and Coons. He got a bullet in me, too. You all saw how I barely made it back here alive. I say it's time we get up a rope party and string him up for what he done!'

'Now wait just a minute,' Buckner shouted over the buzz of the room. 'Keen has been through here before and he's never been any kind of trouble like that. What you're saying doesn't make any sense to me.'

'Maybe Peet is right,' another man shouted from one of the tables. 'He was out there, he ought to know what happened.'

'I'm telling you there isn't going to be any vigilante hanging now or any other time. Peet, if you've got something to settle with Keen, do it on your own. Don't come in here trying to rile everyone else up and start a riot. You and your pals here better watch your step or you might start something you can't finish. Keen keeps pretty much to himself. You push him very far and there'll be gun play, and you're the one who'd end up dead.'

'What kind of town is this?' Burl turned away from the bar facing the room, hands on his hips. 'You want to let a murderer like Keen walk around town all high and mighty like he never shot down innocent men like dogs? You're all going to be sorry if you don't help me settle this right now tonight.' He grabbed Heck and Minx, pushing them towards the front door. 'If anyone in here is with me, meet me outside!'

But one of the teenage boys in the wagon train named Eddy Casner had sneaked away from his father's wagon to see the sights of town that night. While Peet ranted and raved, Eddy stood outside the saloon, peeking around the front door listening to every word. When Peet started across the room for the door, young Eddy turned and ran up the street as fast as he could, back towards the wagon camp. He had to tell Will Keen what he'd heard, although he also knew he stood to get a whipping from his dad for sneaking away when he was supposed to be sleeping with his family.

Will and Wrangel stood outside

Foot's wagon talking when Eddy ran up wide-eyed and out of breath. 'Mr Keen!' He barely got the words out gasping for air.

'What is it, boy?' Will turned to the youngster's sudden intrusion.

'I was down in town and I heard this man in a bar say they should come up here and try to hang you. So I ran back here to warn you about it. When my paw finds out I'm going to get the belt for sure!'

'*Hang* me, what man said that, son?'

Wrangel leaned down and put a hand on Eddy's shoulder, trying to calm him down. 'Now slow down, boy. You can't go around making up stories like this. You're letting your imagination run wild. You didn't really hear any one say that, did you?'

'I sure did, Mr Foot. I wouldn't make up something like this. I'm already in enough trouble for sneaking out. I sure ain't gonna tell a lie too. Look,' Eddy pointed at men carrying flaming torches coming up the street. 'They're coming after you Mr Keen, just like I said!'

Will and Wrangel turned to see a dozen men lit by firelight marching closer with Burl Peet in the lead. At first Will didn't recognize Peet because of the flickering play of light, but as he came closer shouting and pointing, he finally did.

'I'm getting my shotgun. I never put a gun on any man in my life, but I am tonight. I'm not going to allow any lynching of anyone, least of all you, Will,' Wrangel announced, quickly climbing into his wagon and disappearing in the back as Dolores' sleepy voice could be heard asking what he was doing.

'Don't get involved in this. I'll handle it myself!' Will called after him, but without a reply.

Peet and his mob of noisy men stopped thirty feet away brandishing their torches, with Burl's voice rising above the others. 'That's him, that's the half breed murderer I told you killed my friends,' he pointed. 'I say let's string him up right now before he and them sod busters he's leading can make a run for it. He got away with it once. We're not going to give him a second chance to gun down innocent people, are we!'

'We're with you, Peet,' one man in the crowd shouted. 'Let's get a rope on him and get to it!'

Wrangel suddenly emerged from the back of the wagon with a double-barrel shotgun. Standing in front of the wagon seat he levelled the wicked scattergun on the crowd of men, pulling both hammers back full cock. 'I swear as God is my witness, the first man who tries to take one more step forward is going get the taste of both barrels loaded with buckshot. I ain't talking through my hat, either. All of you better believe me!'

'Stay out of it, Wrangel,' Will tried to dissuade him again. 'Take care of Dolores and Sarah. I'll take deal with Peet in my own way.'

'Not this time, Will. I won't stand for something like this.'

Keen stepped forward to his right, moving away from the wagon, but never taking his eyes off Peet. The crowd behind Peet suddenly grew quiet, eyeing Wrangel and his shotgun threat. Several men began slowly backing up, realizing they might have bitten off more than they could chew.

Will's hand moved down until he was comfortably touching the butt of his six gun. 'You're a yellow liar, Peet, but if it's a showdown you want, I'll give you one. Step away from the rest of those men so they don't catch a bullet. You got away once out in the desert after you and your pals tried to raid the wagons. This time it's just you and me.'

Peet's eyes went from Keen to Wrangel who was still holding his shotgun on the remaining men. He heard the rustle of feet behind him. Turning, he saw Heck and Minx backpeddling further down the street, as more men abandoned him. Several more wagon drivers came into sight from their wagons, wondering what all the shouting was about. Wrangel warned them not to get involved, until one pointed at Peet. 'That's one of the men who tried to rob us out in the desert!' he shouted.

'Yeah, I remember him too!' another driver exclaimed. 'He ought to be in jail for what he and the other two with him tried to do.'

More torch carriers began walking back, realizing they'd been duped by Peet's lies and wild story. When he turned around again, he stood alone facing Keen, with a sinking feeling in his stomach as the fire of revenge suddenly burned out and fear took its place.

'Make your move, Peet. This is going to end right here and now,' Will's voice was low, steady and insistent.

For a moment there was only dead silence before Burl Peet found his voice again. He slowly raised both hands empty of a weapon. 'I'm not taking on a double-barrelled shotgun and you too.' His voice shook with emotion, and he dropped the coiled rope in his hands, stepping back. 'But I ain't forgetting it either. Another time and another place it'll all turn out different. You'll see, Keen.'

Wrangel lowered his shotgun as Peet and the last of the mob retreated down the street into the night, leaving their torches dying on muddy ground. Foot took in a deep breath as his wife and Sarah stepped into the front of the wagon with blankets wrapped over their nightgowns.

'Are you all right, dear?' Dolores put her arm around Wrangel, as Sarah did the same while looking at Will holstering his wheel gun, looking back up at her.

'I am, but look,' he held out his hand still quivering with emotion. 'I almost shot a man tonight. I've never done anything like this before. The Good Book says there is never an excuse for taking a human life, but I was ready to do it. Even Will tried to stop me, but I was still ready to pull the trigger. I don't ever want to go that far again.'

'Are you OK, Will?' Sarah asked as he came up to the wagon resting his hands on the sideboards.

'Yes, I am, but I know we haven't seen the last of Burl Peet, not after what he tried to do here tonight. Somewhere, at some time, he'll be back to try again — but next time I hope it's just him and me, and that he leaves everyone else out of it. I don't want anyone in this wagon train involved or hurt, and that especially goes for you and your mom and dad. Wrangel tried to help me, but it was a dangerous thing for him to do. I believe now the best thing for all of us is to pull out of here early in the morning. Nothing good can come of staying any longer. Wrangel, let everyone know we're leaving, and thanks for what you tried to do. Just promise me you won't do it again. This wagon train needs you up front leading it, not wounded or worse.'

Grey cloudy skies were barely coloured with the first light of dawn when Will Keen saddled up Blue alongside Wrangel's wagon. He pulled a bandana up over his nose against the cold, before turning to Foot, who was already in the seat, reins in hands.

'You ready?' he asked.

'You bet, Will. Lead us on out of here and let's put Cedarville as far behind us as we can. I don't want to see another hellacious confrontation like we did last night.'

'Neither do I, if we can help it.'

The muffled rumble of twenty-three wagons beginning to roll through thick slush of mud and snow left the town still sleeping soundly under heavy blankets and cold stoves. When the fullness of day lit the mountain town hours later, the first businessmen bundled in heavy clothes appeared on Main Street unlocking their stores. The first thing they noticed was that the big wagon lot at the end of town stood empty. Only deep wheel tracks in the snow were left to show the pioneers had ever been there. Without their flurry of buying goods and supplies, the businesses' last chance for sales before hard winter set in disappeared in those same empty wheel tracks. The bitterness about Burl Peet's failed hanging party slowly faded away too, only rein-forcing the general opinion of most people in town that he was still a loud-mouth troublemaker and someone too danger-ous to challenge.

In the run-down shack just outside Cedarville, Peet, Heck and Minx shivered under thin wool blankets each night, constantly having to go out each day to gather enough wood to keep their small stove fired up to keep them from freezing to death. Four days had passed since the wagons pulled out, when one morning Burl ordered Minx to go to town to buy more food to restock their dwindling supply.

'Tell Heck to go, will ya,' Zack moaned. 'I don't want to have to walk through all that snow. My feet will freeze wearing these worn-out boots of mine.'

'Oren can go next time. You want to eat tonight, you get to it or starve to death. I'm paying to feed both of you. Don't forget that, and stop crying about it.'

Minx pulled on his coat and hat

exiting the shack slamming the door behind him, shoving both hands in his pocket still mumbling to himself. Thirty minutes later he stepped through the door of Dawson's, stamping snow off his feet. The pot-belly stove in the middle of the room was already crackling, glowing cheery red radiating heat. He went to it warming numb hands, as Dawson came out of the back room eyeing his first customer of the day.

'What can I do for you, Minx?' He asked. 'You're up early today.'

'Here's a list of stuff Peet wrote down.' He handed the paper over. 'I think it's got bacon, beans, some flour and a few other things. I'm staying right here by this stove while you go get it. I'm so cold I can't even feel my feet any more.'

Dawson went about the store filling the order while talking over his shoulder. 'I don't imagine that old shack you're staying in keeps out much cold, does it? It looks like you could throw a cat through the walls.'

'Yeah, it's pretty thin for sure, but it's a whole lot better than a tent. Seems pretty quiet here in town.'

'It is since those wagon people pulled out.'

'You mean they ain't up at the end of town? When did they leave?'

'Let's see. I guess it's been about three or maybe four days ago. I was real sorry to see them go. Lost a lot of business when they rolled out.'

'You better hurry up with those groceries. I've got to get back to the shack real quick.'

'What's your hurry? This is the warmest place you'll be all day. Better enjoy it while you can.'

'Nope, I can't. Just finish that list so I can get out of here.'

Zack burst through the door of the shack, red-faced and trying to catch his breath. Heck and Peet turned from the small table next to the stove wondering why he was breathing so hard. Tossing the sack of vitals on the table, he leaned down putting both hands on it supporting himself.

'I got news, and it ain't good,' he blurted out.

'Like what?' Burl asked, leaning back in the chair.

'The whole wagon train already pulled out of town, Dawson said maybe three or four days ago. I knew you'd want to know about that real fast, Burl. That's why I ran back up here.'

Peet's face dropped. 'Three or four days ago, are you sure?'

'That's what he said. Everyone figured they'd stay around longer, resting up their animals before moving on, but they lit out instead.'

'We're going after them. I'm not finished with that half breed scout of theirs, not by a long shot!'

'What do you mean, we?' Heck spoke up. 'We don't have no beef with Keen. We tried to help you out once, and that didn't work. Besides, we'd likely freeze to death out there trying to catch up to them. This snow is gonna keep piling up!'

'I said you two are going. Start getting your gear together and shut up about it!'

*   *   *

The wagon teams laboured slowly higher day by day, climbing for the final mountain top pass with Will always in the lead breaking trail, searching for the old wagon road buried in fresh snow. Since leaving Cedarville he'd driven the wagoneers hard, relentlessly trying to top high country before more snow fell, blocking the trail and closing it for the entire winter.

But even with all the problems and worries he had each day keeping the wagons together and people's hopes up, in the back of his mind he had still not forgotten about Burl Peet's failed attempt to sick a lynch mob on him. It was clear Peet had done everything he could to avenge the deadly shoot-out back in the desert. But would he still continue to try even with Cedarville now far behind him? That question always lingered on Keen's mind.

Once over the final barrier of the Cascades and down the other side, lush valleys, warmer temperatures, rich soil awaiting the bite of a plough, all waited the arrival of the brave men and women in those wagons behind him. He had to get them there, and nothing else must stop him. Not even the chance that death might somehow be someplace ahead waiting to end all those dreams.

★   ★   ★

Three riders bundled up in all the clothes they could wear, took up the trail out of town following deep wagon ruts now frozen in snow. Burl Peet rode in the lead, occasionally twisting in the saddle, checking to be sure his two unhappy pals were still behind him. Heck rode second with Minx bringing up the rear, and good thing he was, because Peet couldn't hear his constant complaining to Heck. Even Oren got tired of it, turning around time after time telling him to be quiet. The third night on the trail the trio sat shivering around a wet, sputtering fire with Zack eyeing his pals mournfully while Peet untied a sack of hardtack, venison jerky and dried corn kernels. Taking out a handful, he passed the sack to Heck who did the same, then Minx, who refused to take any of it.

'No man can last out here eating that stuff,' he moaned, tossing the sack back to Peet. 'We need some red meat to keep from freezing to death out here.'

'The only red meat we're going to get is in those wagons once we catch up to them. You better eat what I brought or starve to death. I don't care which one, but you better be ready with that six-gun when we do.'

'We've been trailing them for three days,' Heck broke in. 'I'd'a thought by now we'd have them in sight. Instead all we see is more snow each day. Maybe they're too far ahead to ever get close?'

'Don't talk like a damn fool. We'll see

them either tomorrow or the next day. Use your head besides something to put a hat on. Those wagons can't move fast or very far each day, and we can. When we do catch up we'll circle out ahead of them and take Keen with rifles when he rides into view. He'll never know what hit him, and no one will ever find his body until the spring thaw, if mountain lions don't find him first and scatter his bones!'

7

A dozen wagon drivers stood hunched against the cold, facing a roaring camp fire, warming their hands as dawn framed the black silhouette of jagged mountain tops not far to the west. A glance at that final barrier showed wind-driven clouds with an icy gleam moving fast over the tops, promising more snow on the way. Will took another sip of his coffee cup before speaking.

'See those tops?' He nodded, the other men turning to follow his stare. 'Once we reach them and go over, it's all downhill from there to Oregon. You'll almost be home by then.'

Wrangel stepped up alongside his trail scout, moved to speak. 'And when we do, we'll all have you to thank for it, Will. I want to say this right now even before we cross over. You've been a friend to all of us, and the most honest man we could have contracted with to get us here across half a nation. You've had to fight off break-downs, thirst, hunger, and even three men who meant to rob us or worse. No man could ask for anyone to do more than you have. I just want you to know how much me and the rest of us here appreciate what you've done.' He slapped Will on the back.

'I've been taking folks like you west for ten years now. I didn't actually plan for it to work out that way, but somehow it did. I'm a man born and bred of this big country, and I guess it couldn't have worked out any other way. After I get all of you safe down to La Grange, my job will be done, and I don't know if I'll take on another wagon outfit or not.'

'Maybe you ought to think about settling down with us, and buy a piece of land?' one driver suggested. 'You're still a young man. You could easily start another life all over again and have plenty of time to do it.'

Will shook his head, a faint smile crossing his face. 'I wouldn't be much of a farmer. I've never really been able to stay in one place for very long without moving again. That's for people like all of you who want to put down roots, grow your crops and families, start new communities. This big country needs folks like you.' He turned to Wrangel. 'I'm going to ride out a little further this morning to see if the trail is still passable with all this snow. Sometimes I might be in sight, and sometimes not. If you don't see me, don't worry about it. You'll be able to follow Blue's tracks easy enough. Just keep on coming.' He glanced east at the awakening sky. 'Here comes tomorrow. Time to hook up your teams. Let's get to it.'

Hidden behind canvas in Foot's wagon, Sarah sat wrapped in a blanket, peeking around the edge, listening to the conversation. She'd never heard Will talk much about himself, and it fascinated her to hear even this little bit. It also strengthened her resolve not to let Will Keen ride away out of her life once they reached La Grange valley, without putting up a fight to tell him exactly how she felt about him. As the impromptu meeting broke up and men started for their wagons, she quietly slid back into a warm pile of blankets, lying down with her eyes wide open, making up plans of her own.

The icy glow of dawn lit another campsite several miles ahead of the wagon train. Burl Peet rolled over, shivering uncontrollably under his thin wool blanket even with the saddle blanket on top of it. Heck stirred restlessly beside him, trying to rub another sleepless night on the trail out of burning eyes. Pulling himself up on one elbow he rolled over trying to focus on his pal, Minx. Only an empty depression showed where Zack had been. Oren blinked, rubbing his eyes harder trying to clear them. When he looked again, a set of footprints led away to where the horses were picketed. Zack Minx had silently slipped away during the night, leaving his two pals on their own.

'Burl — you awake?' Heck asked, sitting up wishing he didn't have to deliver the message he was about to.

Peet made a sound that wasn't really a word.

'You better wake up, and I mean fast. I got some bad news you ain't gonna like.'

Peet groaned, pulling himself upright. 'Like what?'

'Like Zack got up during the night, and lit out on his own. He's gone. It's just you and me, now.'

Peet suddenly whipped off the blanket and staggered to his feet, wild eyed with anger, looking around to be sure Heck knew what he was talking about. He wiped the spittle of rage off his lips with the back of his hand. Pulling his six-gun, he started down the footprints in the snow. At the picket line only two horses stood with steam streaming out of their nostrils at each breath against the icy air.

'That little yellow-bellied coward.

When I catch up to him I'll kill him for this, even if I find him on Main Street in Cedarville!'

Heck came into the clearing with his blanket still wrapped around him, trying to avoid Peet's murderous stare and threats. 'Let 'im go, Burl. He probably wouldn't have been that much help anyway. I'm half froze to death. Why don't we start a fire and try to warm up before we ride out?'

'No, you fool. A fire means smoke you can see a mile away. Get your horse saddled. We've got to get out on the trail where we have a good view. Sooner or later Keen will be coming. If I know him, it'll be sooner. When he does, we'll be waiting, and this time he won't have a shotgun backing him up, either!'

★   ★   ★

Will gave Blue his head only occasionally, reining him up the snow-covered trail in the direction he wanted to go. Horse and rider slowly gained height as

Will's eyes stayed trained on the high ridges ahead, looking for the tell-tale, natural notch where the wagon road went over the top. The first weak rays of sun began lighting the land, bringing everything into sharp focus against a glistening background of white. Keen turned in the saddle to see if the wagons were still in sight. They were not, but he knew Wrangel would be coming on making the best time he could.

Ahead of Will a low rocky outcrop topped in brush and snow-laden pines cut across the trail at an angle. A low spot in its middle marked the wagon road's path through. Without warning Blue suddenly came to a stop, ears pricked forward. He snorted, staring at the low ridge a hundred yards ahead.

'What is it, boy?' Will whispered in the animal's ear. 'What do you see, huh?'

He leaned slightly forward to pull his rifle from its scabbard. Those few inches saved his life as rifle shots shattered the morning air, bullets whizzing by just over his shoulder. Two blossoms of blue gun smoke stained the morning air, marking the hideout of the ambushers. Will dug his heels hard and fast into Blue's flanks, leaning low in the saddle on an all-out run towards the lower end of the rocky shelf as more rifle fire exploded. Reaching cover he baled out of the saddle, rifle in hand, slapping Blue hard on the rump to keep him running ahead as a decoy to draw the attention of the shooters.

Keen didn't have the time to wonder why or who was trying to kill him: he had to see the shooters before they saw him, moving at a run up the timbered cover. Nearing the wagon road notch, he heard the sound of horses pounding away fast. Breaking out of cover he saw two riders fleeing, snow flying from their horses' hoofs. Oren Heck twisted in the saddle wildly firing his revolver. Will swung his rifle up, and at the roar of his shot, Heck threw up his hands and tumbled backwards off the running horse, crashing into the snow without moving. Keen swung the rifle ahead on

Peet, just as he disappeared into another stand of pines out of sight. Will quickly turned, putting two fingers on his lips, whistling loudly for Blue. A moment later the big horse came running out of cover towards him.

Peet savagely whipped his horse on a frantic run until the animal began struggling to keep pace through deepening snow. Fear clutched Peet's body, his breath coming in short gasps, his heart pounding as if it would explode out of his chest. The first time he looked back he saw he was riding alone. Moments later when he looked again he saw Keen riding low in the saddle, quickly gaining ground on him. Desperate not to be caught, he pulled his rifle from its scabbard and began swinging it down like a club on the horse's flanks, trying to beat the last ounce of energy out of the faltering animal, until it finally stumbled and fell, sending him flying face first into the snow, nearly knocking him unconscious.

He coughed and sputtered, trying to

spit snow from his mouth and nose, staggering upright. His rifle, where was it? Ten feet away he spied the stock sticking up out of the snow as Will rode in, leaping off Blue even before the big horse had come to a stop. Peet lunged for it, falling to his knees, but Will cut him off, pulling his six-gun, standing over the top of him.

'It's just you and me now. You've got a pistol. Get to your feet and use it. I don't want to kill you on your knees begging for your life. Get up!'

Burl couldn't speak — his mouth hung half open, his eyes locked on Keen like a bird hypnotized, seeing a snake about to strike. More seconds passed as he tried regaining his senses. He slowly felt for the pistol. It was still in its holster. All he had to do was stand up and pull it, taking a chance he'd beat the trail scout. Just as quick he decided he couldn't outpull Will Keen. Instead, he tried something else to save himself.

'I'm — all broke up inside. My horse

threw me — I can't feel my hands.'

'You better get up and pull it. I won't ask again.'

'I can't, I tell ya'. You want to gun down a cripple — you'll hang for it. That's what'll happen to you. Go ahead and shoot!' Peet, still on his knees, held up both hands as the first wagons came into view, lumbering towards the two men.

'See, there are even witnesses. You can't kill me now. Even your friends won't stand for it. They'll all turn against you!' Peet screamed defiantly.

Will heard the rattle of wagons coming closer. Stepping back he turned to see Wrangel up front, whipping his team closer. He gritted his teeth. Peet was right: he'd been saved by the very pioneers he was ready to rob and shoot down in cold blood out in the high desert weeks earlier. Will leaned down and grabbed Peet by his jacket, pulling him up to his feet, nose to nose.

'Your time is still coming. When it is, I'll be the one to end it,' he hissed through clenched teeth. 'No one will save you next time.'

'Will, what's going on? Who have you got there?' Wrangel called out. The big Conestoga pulled to a squeaky stop, with Dolores and Sarah on the seat next to Wrangel while the rest of the wagons pulled into view. Foot stood staring down at the two men. Suddenly he remembered the face of Burl Peet.

'Why, that's one of the murderers you fought with back in the desert. He's the same man who tried to start that hanging party back in Cedarville, too! What's he doing way out here, Will?'

'Him and another man tried to bushwhack me. The other one is lying back in the snow. You just saved this one by showing up, or he'd be too.'

'You killed the other one?'

'I did, before he could kill me.'

Peet saw his chance to save himself further, eyeing the two women, sounding as pitiful as possible. 'My horse threw me — I'm all broke up inside. I need help real bad — before this madman kills me. You're all good

Christian people, aren't you? Help me! Don't let him shoot me down like a dog!'

Will still kept Peet tight in his grip. Reaching down he pulled Peet's pistol, tossing it in the snow, as more drivers abandoned their wagons and walked up to see why they were stopped, until everyone was talking at the same time asking questions.

'Listen to me,' Will shouted over all of them. 'This man tried to ambush me. His crying is all an act. There's nothing wrong with him except I caught up to him. I'd take him back to Cedarville, and let vigilantes take care of him, but I can't. We're too close to topping out, and I don't want to stop and turn back now.'

'Then what else can we do?' Wrangel questioned, as the other men nodded in agreement. 'We can't just turn him loose after what he tried to do.'

Everyone began talking again, arguing about how to handle the strange situation. As disagreement grew, Peet

152

saw another chance to try to save himself. He broke into the conversation, shouting above everyone else.

'You just heard what your scout said. You can't go back to town and have to keep on going. The only answer is to turn me loose. It's my word against Keen's anyway. He shot down my partner without even a call. He's lying dead back there in the snow. Keen even said so himself. He'd be the one who'll get himself hung, not me!'

The discord grew until Wrangel, standing in the wagon seat, shouted over everyone to quiet down. As arguments subsided, he began speaking.

'I think I've got an idea that might work.'

'What is it?' one driver in the crowd questioned.

'I say we take this man with us and let the law in La Grange take care of him. That's the only way any of this makes sense. We can all testify what he tried to do both back in the desert and in town. That ought to be enough to put him away behind bars for a long time. Will told me some time back the town is big enough so they've got to have some law. That's the only thing that makes sense to me.'

Peet saw his chances sinking just when he thought he'd talked himself free. He had to say something, and fast.

'You bible thumpers want me riding in your wagons with all them pretty women and young girls, do you?' He eyed Dolores and Sarah, with a leering smile for emphasis. 'You'd have to stay up all day and all night watching me like a hawk, if I'm half as bad as Keen says I am. Who wants to be first to volunteer to take me in? I'd love a nice warm bed and wagon ride, instead of freezing to death out here. Step right up. I'm ready!' He boldly challenged them all, raising his voice.

Will saw the look of confusion on everyone's face, including Wrangel. He knew he had to stop this madness now. Pulling Peet up close again he whispered in his ear. 'I know how to handle you,' he hissed, before turning to the crowd of men.

'He's going to ride up front with me on point. I'll tie his hands behind his back so he doesn't get any ideas about trying to ride away. I'll keep an eye on him all the way to La Grange. That solves this problem real fast.'

'You sure you can do that?' Wrangel questioned, looking around, unsure, at the other men, who were all wondering the same thing.

'I am. The law is the only answer to take care of this murdering snake. We've got plenty of spare horses. I'll put him on one, and we can get going again. That's enough talk about it. Get me a horse and rope.'

'You can't do this to me,' Peet screamed. 'Don't let this half breed treat me like a dog. I'm a man, not some kind of animal!'

Keen still had a grip on Peet's jacket, and slammed him up against Foot's wagon, at arm's length, before turning back to the men. 'We're leaving with him riding up front, like I said. The only difference is, now I have two reasons for getting all of you to La Grange. I might even stay long enough to watch this back-stabber get put behind bars!'

Tying Peet's hands behind his back, Will bodily boosted the still protesting killer on to a horse, before saddling up himself. He led Peet's horse by a bridle rope so he had no control of the animal whatsoever. As wagons and riders started again for the tops, Burl Peet was still complaining loudly — but Will ignored him until finally he ran out of breath and went quiet.

* * *

Late in the afternoon of the following day, Will reached the high pass at the top of the Cascade Range. He pulled both horses to a stop and looked back at the line of wagons slowly labouring higher. Waving his hand over his head in a circle, he signalled to Wrangel Foot in the lead wagon that at last they had finished the long, wearying climb. Peet meanwhile sat glumly in the saddle still trying to think of some way to break free and escape. Then the answer came to him in an instant, and half a hidden smile suddenly came over his face: night-time, that was it. When everyone else was asleep, including Keen, he'd try to free himself and slip away unheard and unseen. Even Keen had to sleep, didn't he? Night-time was the one time when the cards were dealt in his favour. He figured it was at least another six or seven days before reaching La Grange. That would give him plenty of time to take a chance to try for it. Peet sat back in the saddle smiling grimly to himself. At last he had a plan — now all he needed was the right time to pull it off. With a little extra luck he might even be able to kill Will Keen before he left.

The first night after the wagon train had topped the mountains and started on the downhill slope, every pioneer in those wagons was jubilant with their success. Men, women and children gathered around cooking fires talking excitedly about finally reaching La Grange valley, and how they would start their new homesteads. Will stood watching Dolores and Sarah cooking over a big cast-iron pot suspended over a crackling fire on a three-legged stand. Wrangel sat nearby thoughtfully smoking his pipe, Peet on the ground up against a wagon wheel, hands tied in front of him so he could eat. Every time Sarah glanced at their dangerous guest, he made some kind of face back at her pursing his lips in a quiet kiss, or winking. She moved around the fire putting her back to him, which only brought a quiet laugh under his breath.

Will had worked out a schedule with Wrangel about how to guard Peet each night. The original plan was for the wagon leader to sit up with their prisoner after dinner until midnight, when Will would take over until dawn. But two days using that plan made it clear to Keen he would have to change it, as he found himself the next day almost falling asleep in the saddle from so little sleep. He told Foot they'd reverse the roles, and if Foot found himself getting drowsy during the day he could have Dolores or Sarah take the reins for a while so he could rest a bit or catch a quick nap. Both women were capable of controlling the animals for a few hours each day, tough as it was.

Each night Wrangel, Dolores and Sarah slept in the wagon. Will didn't want Peet any closer to them than absolutely necessary, so he and Peet slept on a canvas under the wagon with blankets on top. The only way to be certain Peet stayed put each night was to tie his hands behind his back again, and his feet on a short rope to one of the wagon wheels. He complained bitterly he'd lost all feeling in his hands and feet, but Will wouldn't change it. When he went to sleep after checking the ropes were secured, Will still slept uneasily with his six-gun close against him in quick reach.

The fourth evening after eating dinner, the fire next to Wrangel's wagon burned lower as Dolores and Sarah climbed into the wagon, saying good night to Foot and Keen. Will sat up a little while longer talking to the wagon man about tomorrow's ride further downhill, and when he expected to reach La Grange. Peet sat on the ground tied up, as usual, listening to all this without ever uttering a word. He'd already decided this was the night to try and make his break for freedom. It didn't matter if he had to kill anyone to pull it off. This was his one chance: he had to take it. Keen spread out the canvas under the wagon and blankets, ordering Peet to crawl in, then tying his feet to the wagon wheel. Sliding in next to him he pulled his six-gun close.

An hour passed as the fire burned lower. Wrangel sat on a folding stool smoking his pipe, shotgun over his lap, feeding a few small pieces of wood into the snapping flames to keep some heat radiating from it. In another half hour he began to tire, rubbing his eyes and fighting to stay awake, while Peet silently worked at the rope binding his hands, watching Foot intently, peeking out from under the blanket. At first the knot held tight, but slowly, by twisting and turning, it began to give a bit. Thirty minutes later Wrangel's head dropped, half awake, half asleep. While Peet worked to free his hands, the more the overpowering urge to sleep worked on Foot: he sat with eyes closed, breathing more and more slowly until he lost the battle against fatigue and lack of sleep.

Suddenly Peet felt the knot loosen, freeing his hands at last, the rush of blood bringing back feeling as he lay there smiling to himself. Inch by precious inch his hands moved down to the knotted rope around his boots. This time using both hands the knot came untied faster. He rested a moment, gaining strength and figuring out his next move. Foot was sound asleep. He was the target, to get that shotgun.

Keen, closer to him, was the real problem. Burl knew he had to slide out from under covers and get that scattergun before the trail scout woke. Once he got his hands on that double barrel, he could cover both men: nothing could stop him then. If either tried, he had two ugly black barrels loaded with buckshot that could cut a man in two at this murderous range.

Peet craw-fished out from under the blanket and wagon until he was clear. Foot was only ten short feet away on the other side of a glowing pile of coals in the fire pit. Peet started crawling ever so slowly towards him, his heart beating like a drum. His diabolical plan was working perfectly, and he was only seconds away from completing it. Pulling himself up alongside the snoring man he picked up a large rock, rising like a dark shadow, hand poised high over Wrangel's head. With one swinging blow he struck Foot, driving him backwards off the stool on to the ground. Foot gave a muffled cry of pain and for help, as the shotgun clattered away across the ground.

Burl lunged for the weapon, struggling to get both hands on it, while Foot, nearly unconscious, wrapped his arms around Peet's legs, trying to stop him. Peet got his hands on the shotgun, fighting to pull both hammers back with one hand while trying to beat Wrangel off him with the other. He finally kicked the old man off, and lurched to his feet. But as he swung the scattergun around, Keen came over the top of him, crashing the barrel of his six-gun down on Burl's head, knocking him nearly unconscious. As Burl went down he pulled off one barrel, the explosive lead pellets shredding a ragged hole through the canvas on the side of the wagon. Dolores's cry of terror from inside the wagon only heightened the tension in this vicious battle for life or death.

Somehow Wrangel stumbled to his feet, blood running down his face from the open gash on his head. Falling on top of Peet he held him down while Will ran to retrieve ropes, quickly tying Burl's hands and feet again. Foot staggered upright, and walked unsteadily to the wagon, calling out groggily for his wife and daughter. Dolores and Sarah appeared from under the canvas, wide-eyed with fear and confusion.

'Are — either — of you hurt?' he called out, grabbing the side of the wagon to keep himself from going down. Both women came swiftly out of the wagon and wrapped their arms around him to keep him standing.

'We're both all right, Wrangel,' Dolores's face twisted in shock at the sight of her husband's blood-spattered face. 'My God, what happened, are you wounded? Sit down so I can help you. Sarah, get some cloth and soak it in water, quick!'

Will dragged Burl Peet up against the wagon and pulled him up into a sitting position, and looped a rope around his chest then back through the wooden spokes of the wheel, tying it tightly. 'From now until we reach La Grange, this is how you're going to sleep each night, so get used to it.'

Burl didn't answer. He sat head down, eyes closed, his head still ringing from the blow of Will's six-gun. But one thing he was certain of, and that was, he'd never get a second chance to break free again.

8

The long line of wagons slowly descended, leaving snowy, timbered peaks in their wheel tracks, the land ahead changing into little open valleys with rounded hilltops over the next five days. Excited anticipation of what lay ahead was obvious in the faces, talk and attitude of all the pioneers, knowing their worst days were finally behind them, while searching ahead for that first glimpse of La Grange.

Wrangel Foot sat in the lead wagon, head bandaged, stubbornly refusing to give up the reins to let his wife or daughter take over while he rested in the back. The pounding misery of his head wound never seemed to end. He and all the pioneers had fought their way west for over two months over icy mountains, across smouldering deserts and fording swollen rivers. He wasn't about to miss seeing these last miles come to an end. He'd vowed when the wagons clattered down the main street in La Grange, he meant to be in the lead regardless of how miserable he felt. There was no two ways about that.

Will rode ahead pulling Peet's horse, with Burl's hands still tied behind him. His complaints and threats began to rise again, realizing they were getting close to La Grange. Keen still ignored him. At mid-morning, seven days after crossing the high pass in the mountains, Will reined to a halt at the end of a long plateau. Gazing downhill into a broad valley ahead, multi colored dots of houses and stores winked back at him through scattered timber. At last La Grange lay only two more miles away. Peet was quick to react.

'Soon as we get to town I'm getting me a good lawyer,' he snorted. 'You think you got me hung, but I'm far from it. You're the one who might end up wearing a rope necktie.'

Will glanced at his murderous companion without answering. Instead the sound of heavy wagons coming closer got his attention, until Wrangel pulled his team to a stop, standing in the seat as his horses snorted their relief.

'There it is,' Will nodded ahead. 'You and your people are just about home, unless some might want to go ahead into the Willamette valley a bit farther west.'

'Some might. I've heard a few mention it. I'll have to get everyone together and ask what they want to do, once we get into town. It's a beautiful sight after all these months, I'll tell you that for sure. What about Peet, here?'

'I'll take him to the sheriff's office. Last time I was through here John Skinner was the lawman. Whether he still is or not I'll have to find out. No matter who it is, Peet's going straight into a jail cell. His days on the loose are over.'

'That's what you think, half breed,' Peet shouted back, spitting a stream of spittle at Will. 'As long as I'm alive and breathing I'll have the chance to finish you off, and don't ever forget it!'

Will pulled Peet's horse up close. He'd had all the threats and foul language he could stand. Reaching over he grabbed Burl by his shirt collar, twisting it so tight his face turned red and his eyes bulged out.

'You keep your dirty little mouth shut in front of these women, or I'll break your worthless neck,' Keen hissed, pulling Peet nose to nose.

'Don't break his neck, Will,' Foot called out. 'Let the law do that at the end of a rope. Let's get down there and see what some real civilization looks like. God knows it's been a real long time coming.'

People on the street saw the long line of white-topped Conestogas descending the plateau long before they reached town. By the time Will rode into town down the main street, pulling Peet's horse behind him, the rattle of wagons and clatter of horses' hoofs had curious onlookers lining both sides of the street. Some shouted greetings, a few tipped their hats, others only waved, watching the canvas caravan roll past, eyeing all the pioneers looking back at them. Will gave Foot directions where he could park the wagons just outside town, while he took Peet and headed for the sheriff's office.

*   *   *

'Hey, John,' a man on the street called out to Skinner. 'That wagon scout was down at your office looking for you a few minutes ago. He had some man with him all tied up like a roasting pig, too.'

'Thanks, I'll head down there and see what's going on.' Skinner tipped his hat, striding toward his office two blocks away.

La Grange's sheriff was a man who generally did not have to deal with the serious problems of law enforcement that other frontier towns did. There was no mining or timber business to attract the kind of rough, rowdy, sometimes dangerous men who worked in those back-breaking jobs, then blew off steam on Saturday and Sunday nights, drinking heavily, brawling, or threatening gunplay to satisfy their frustration fed by endless hard labour. Instead, La Grange was largely peopled by farmers, cattlemen, their growing families and store owners in town. The very first building to go up when the town was founded was not a saloon, but a church, and the second was a school. Whiskey parlours only came later.

Skinner was a man who also believed in the Good Book, practising its admonitions, wearing a badge out on the street and at home. He knew Will Keen from previous years, bringing new settlers into Oregon Territory. If Will wanted to see him, he had to have a good reason. Skinner's long legs carried him swiftly down the street until his office came into view up ahead. Keen was still there, holding another man by the back of his belt, hands tied behind his back.

'What have you got there, Keen?' The sheriff came up, eyeing both men.

'A bushwhacker and backshooter. Likely a murderer more than once, too. He and a pal tried to ambush me back over the mountains while I was leading the wagons out from Cedarville.'

'Where's the other one to?'

'Lying dead up in the snow. I stopped him first. Mountain lions or wolves will take care of what's left of him. I was too busy trying to catch this one to care.'

'You have any witnesses to all this?' Skinner looked Burl Peet up and down suspiciously.

'Yes, a whole wagon train full of people. They'll tell you what happened. You might want to start with their leader, Wrangel Foot.'

'I'll do just that, but first let's get this character inside into a cell.'

'This half breed's a liar, can't you see that? He even killed two of my friends!' Burl shouted, as the sheriff opened the door and pushed him inside. 'I want a lawyer, too. Be sure I get one, you hear?'

Skinner glanced at Keen. A grim smile briefly crossed his face. Walking Peet to a cell, he motioned him inside, clanging the steel door shut behind him, then ordered him to back up to the bars so he could untie his hands.

'Remember what I said about that lawyer,' Burl insisted again.

'We don't have a lawyer here in La Grange. The nearest one might be over in Baker City, and I'm not about to take the time to ride all the way over there to find out.'

'I don't stand a chance against a wagonload of liars. They'll all go for Keen just to get rid of me!'

'We have a circuit judge who comes through here twice a year. You'll have to take your chances in front of him.'

Burl's mouth fell open and his eyes narrowed. He gripped the cold steel bars with both hands so tight his knuckles turned white.

'When was the last time he came through?'

'About two months ago. It'll probably be another three or four before he does again.' Skinner stared back waiting for a reaction.

'You can't do this to me,' Peet shook the bars violently, his stare turning to

Keen. 'That half breed will say anything to try to keep me locked up. You can't let him get away with it, you hear? He's a liar in white man's clothes. Let me out of here and give me a pistol. I'll face him down right now, and all you'll need is an undertaker to put him away when I'm done. Open up this damn cell door, I tell you!'

Skinner escorted Will back outside closing the door behind him to block out the yelling. 'He's not going anyplace for a while. When Judge Deen shows up he'll likely put him away for twenty years.'

'He's dangerous and smart. Don't underestimate him. Underneath all that yelling is a cold-blooded killer. He's done a lot more of it than just trying to ambush me up in the mountains.'

'I'll keep an eye on him, you don't have to worry about that. I can see he does have a special kind of hate for you, though.'

'I know that. I could have ended it up in the snow. Maybe I should have.'

'No, you did the right thing, bringing

him down here. Once he's in territorial prison, he'll likely never leave it alive. They've got a big bone-yard out back filled with what's left of men like him. If you'll be taking some of these wagon people on to the Willamette Valley, I'll take your statement down in writing to be used in court. Along with your people who'll settle here, it will be enough for a guilty verdict for sure. Do you think you'll be back next year with another wagon train?'

'I haven't thought much about that yet. I'm really not sure what I'll do. Maybe a little time away from it might decide that.'

'Whatever you do, it's always good to see you again.' Skinner stuck out his hand, and both men shook. 'Take care of yourself, Will. And don't worry about Burl Peet. I'll take care of him for you, too.'

Wrangel Foot had his hands full the remainder of that week, learning which families were decided to stay in La Grange, registering for a new homestead, and which were determined to make the last leg of the journey to Willamette Valley, with Keen leading them there. Will gave Sheriff Skinner the sworn statement he'd asked for, including an account of the first thwarted attack on the wagon train made by Peet and his pals back in the desert. Wrangel witnessed the statement, and added his own thoughts for Skinner.

'If me and my family had decided to stay here, I'd be the first man up on that witness stand to testify against that murderer,' he assured the sheriff. 'If it wasn't for this man,' he nodded toward Will, 'some of us would never have made it this far.'

'I understand. There is one thing you can do for me before you leave. I'd like the names of other families in your wagon train that I can use for witnesses when Judge Deen comes through here.'

'I'll be glad to do that. I know they'll all be more than willing to back up what Will has said. Peet's a killer. There's no doubt about that in the mind of anyone in this wagon train. It looks from my count that about half of us are going on, but that still leaves plenty of people for you to choose from when the trial takes place. I'll also take the time to introduce you to some of them before we pull out.'

'I appreciate your help. I want to be certain Peet gets a sentence that puts him away for years, or maybe even a hangman's rope. Judge Deen is a hard-nosed old hand when it comes to the law. They don't call him the 'hanging judge' for no reason. He means to make this big country civilized for people, no matter how much rope it takes. Some even joke he carries a thick coil of rope around in the back of his buckboard for just that purpose, but never to his face.'

★   ★   ★

Two days after the meeting in Skinner's office, the last wagons rattled down the streets of La Grange for the final leg of their journey to Willamette Valley. Will, riding Blue in the lead, looked back

177

over his shoulder to see Wrangel first in line as usual, while behind him a dozen other Conestogas followed. Some people on the street waved at the departing pioneers, while others simply stood and watched, wondering what drove so many people to travel a thousand miles in search of a new home none of them had ever seen before.

Someone else was also watching the last wagons roll by: Burl Peet stood atop the hard board bed in his jail cell, pulling himself up by the bars, peering out of a small window. The rattle of the departing wagons and the thudding sound of horses' hoofs drowned out his wild shouts and threats. When the last wagon passed out of sight, Peet dropped back down on the bunk and put his head in both hands, trying to catch his breath, the hate seething up inside him. Keen had won again, but he was still alive. As long as he could draw a breath there was still the slim chance he'd break free and kill that wagon scout one way or the other for what he'd done to him.

* * *

The wagon road to Willamette Valley was well travelled and made easy going for the pioneers, their wagons and animals. In the following five days they reached the broad, rolling expanse that was the fabled valley. Arrowhead-shaped Mount Hood stood gleaming white in snow-clad splendour above the valley, its downhill slopes spreading out like broad fingers on to tree-clad plateaus interspersed with rolling grasslands watered by creeks and streams. Wrangel Foot pulled his team of horses to a stop. Standing in the seat, Dolores and Sarah came up beside him, drinking in the stunning view.

'My God, Mother. Would you just look at this land. It's everything we prayed for, and more. The Good Lord has made it the promised land for all of us!'

Will reined Blue back to Foot's wagon. The look of satisfaction on his face broke into a rare smile. 'Well, Wrangel, you and all your people have finally made it here. I'm glad for all of you.'

'You'll never know how thankful we are, Will. It's just such a magnificent sight it nearly brings me to tears, after what we took the chance to leave behind in Missouri.'

The wagons spread out across the big valley, some families choosing to stake their homestead close to friends, while others sought areas off to themselves. Foot and his family picked a piece of ground close to a fast-running creek and began to lay out plans for a log cabin, barn and corral. Wrangel asked Will if he'd stay on a short time to help him with the heavy work. At first Will said it was best he moved on, but the old man's unflagging insistence made him change his mind. Wrangel thought of Will as much more than only their wagon scout. Although he never said so out loud, he'd grown to think of Will more like the son he and Dolores had lost at birth, years earlier, to consumption. Both he and his wife felt the same way.

Sarah, still enamoured of Will, loved

him staying even for just a short time longer. It didn't take long for her mother to realize her daughter had fallen deeply in love with the quiet man in buckskins, as strange a background as he'd come from. Wrangel, too busy laying out foundations and the hard work that went with it, was oblivious to his daughter's intentions, until one evening after eating dinner when he and Dolores took a walk alone around their homestead.

'You do know by now our daughter is in love with Will, don't you?' She finally broached the subject.

Wrangel stopped walking, turning to look at her with surprise. 'What are you talking about? Do you really believe that?'

'She spends as much time around him as she can every day. Haven't you seen that, dear? Or have you forgotten what love is?'

'Of course I haven't. Don't you accuse me of something like that. You know I love you, don't you? But Sarah is still a . . .'

'Still what, Wrangel? She's no child

any more. Our daughter is nineteen years old and a woman. You do remember how old I was when you asked my mother and father for my hand in marriage, don't you?'

Wrangel tried to ignore the question, still holding Dolores's hands. He didn't know what to say as his mind whirled at the sudden news. All he could think of was questions without answers, and none of those questions were good news. Will meant to leave and move on. He'd said so more than once. Sarah could only be hurt by that. Foot's furrowed brow showed how much concern he suddenly felt for her. 'Let's turn back while I try to make some sense of all this,' he said.

Will didn't know for sure what he'd do or where he'd go once he left the valley. About the only thing he was certain of was he didn't want to take on guiding another wagon train out from back east next spring. It seemed he was always fulfilling the dreams of other people without any of his own. Now, more than ever, it had begun to cause a kind of restlessness and confusion about what to do. He had no family and no close relatives. The only thing that brought back the few pleasant memories he had was recalling his days as a youngster growing up on his mother's ranch back across the Black Rock Desert. After all these years he wondered if anything was left of it, or if it had fallen before the endless advance of Mother Nature. Maybe, he began thinking, he could find himself some peace of mind and a rebirth by making the long, difficult ride back. The more he considered it, the more the idea began to take hold.

Will went down to the creek to fetch two buckets of water one evening as Dolores cooked dinner on an open fire. He'd scooped up the two heavy vessels, one in each hand, and turned around, virtually bumping into Sarah who had quietly stepped up right behind him.

'Sarah.' He took a step back. 'I didn't hear you come up. You must be part Indian.' He tried to make a joke of his surprise.

The young woman came even closer, putting her hands on both his arms, staring him in the face. 'Daddy says you're about to leave. Is that true?'

'Yes, it is. You know I'm not a farmer. I only stayed on to help your dad. Now it's time for me to ride out.'

'Ride out to where? You've got no family, you said so yourself. Where would you go?'

'I ... I'm not real sure yet. Maybe ... '

She suddenly wrapped both hands around his neck, pulling him down and kissing him hard on the lips before letting go. Will's face turned red with embarrassment. He started to put down the buckets to free his hands until she stopped him.

'Don't. I like it when you can't push me away. You ought to know by now that I love you, and have done even when we were back over the mountains. If you do leave you're taking me with you, no matter where you go.'

'Sarah, are you crazy? You can't go

with me. Your folks would never allow it. Where I might end up is no place for any woman to be. Haven't you seen enough hardship out on the trail, to know it's no life for someone like you? Besides, you're just a teenage . . . '

'You listen to me, Will Keen,' she stopped him. 'I'm nineteen years old, and next year I'll be twenty. I'm not some child, and I won't let you call me that. I can ride a horse and run a wagon as good as any man, and you know it. You've seen me do both. I'm not some frilly little schoolgirl. I'm a woman. I've seen how you glanced at me those nights on the trail when we were eating dinner. Open your eyes again, Will!'

For once the wagon scout stood stunned to silence. He slowly lowered both buckets while taking in a deep breath. For the first time ever he reached out, touching her and putting his hands on her shoulders, holding her at arms' length, trying to find the right words to say.

'Listen to me. I know you're not a

child. I didn't mean it that way. I can see you're a young woman and a pretty one, but I couldn't let that get in the way of the job I had to do all these months. We're a dozen years apart in age. How do you think your mother and father would feel about that, and you riding off with a man who has Indian blood in his veins? You've got your family here and a new home to build. This big country needs people like you and your folks settling it. It will be a place for you to marry and raise a family of your own some day. That's the kind of life you should be thinking about, not going off with me to who knows where. I might even go all the way back across the Black Rock to look things over at my mother's old ranch, if there's anything left to look at. I don't have any real plans like everyone else here in this valley. That's no life for you to live, is it?'

'If you had me with you, we could settle any place you like. I don't care where that is. I know what I want.

You've always been alone. Don't you think it's time you considered someone for yourself? I fell in love with you months ago. I know it's real. I know nothing can stand in our way if you'll just see me for what I am, and what we can do together. Do you love me or not? I want an answer right now.'

For once, Will was at a loss for words. All he could do was slowly nod his head, finally admitting his hidden feelings for her. Sarah stepped up close against him and he wrapped his arms around her, knowing he shouldn't, but unable to stop himself.

'Sarah, you don't know what you're asking, to live like I do. Believe me you have no idea.'

'Yes I do. We can do anything together. You'll see!'

9

The four of them — Wrangel, Dolores, Sarah and Will — stood close together talking in serious conversation. Dolores held both her daughter's hands in hers, with tears in her eyes. With Will and Wrangel, it was all man-to-man, eye-to-eye serious conversation. Wrangel reached up, putting a calloused hand on Will's shoulder to emphasize his remarks.

'I'm not sure about all this. I have to tell you that right now, but Sarah insists on it. Her mother and I have tried to talk her out of it, but she can be as stubborn and mule-headed as I am. I guess I've only got myself to blame for that, bringing her up the way we did. You just promise me you'll take care of her and protect her with your life, if that's what it takes. You understand, Will?'

'Of course I do, you and Dolores

don't ever have to worry about that. You and your wife aren't the only ones who tried to change her mind. So did I, and more than once, but we both do want to be together, and this is the only way I can see to do that.'

'I have to tell you it just plain scares me to even think of you two heading back over the mountains through all that snow after what we went through with the wagons. She told us you even want to go all the way back to the Black Rock, too?'

'Yes, that's what I want to do. I'll buy a packhorse once we get back to La Grange, for our gear. Two riders will be able to move a lot faster than we did coming here with all the wagons to worry about.'

'Why not wait and stay here until spring? Mother and I both certainly want to be able to attend your wedding. After all, Sarah is our only child, it's something we've always planned on.'

'I don't want to wait that long. I'm sorry about that, I just don't, Wrangel.

This is something I have to do now. We'll see a justice of the peace and marry in town. It won't be fancy, but it's important to both of us to do it right. I know you and Dolores feel the same way about it even if you won't be there.'

'Some honeymoon.' Wrangel shook his head. 'Climbing back over the Cascades again with all that snow. I sure wish both of you would reconsider.'

'I know it's not easy for you to understand, but I want to get back to my mother's old ranch, or what's left on the site, without waiting for spring. I've thought about it more and more these days. You and Dolores have found the home you've been looking and praying for. You have to try and understand I'm still trying to find mine.'

Dolores pulled her daughter closer talking nearly at a whisper. The fear in her voice was something she could not hide, as she fought to keep from breaking down and making it even more difficult for all four of them. She reached into her pocket and pulled out a small piece of silk cloth with something wrapped up in it.

'This is my mother's wedding ring.' She put it in Sarah's hand. 'I've kept it all these years knowing someday you'd be wearing it too. I never thought it would be passed on in a situation like — this.' Her voice caught in her throat. 'I'm just plain scared, Sarah. I can't hide it. You're going to be far away and I don't know if we'll ever see either of you again.'

'Mom, I'll be all right. Believe me I will. We're both able to do this, I know we are. Maybe next year if everything works out, we can come back for a visit. Please don't cry, or I'll start too. Just remember, Will knows what he's doing, and I'll be all right. You'll see.'

The two women hugged, but Dolores couldn't hold out any longer and she began crying softly under her breath, while Will and her husband locked hands in one last hard stare at each other. 'Remember what I said, Will. Don't let anything happen to our little girl.'

191

'I won't. You've both got my word on it.'

The pair mounted up and started away. Sarah turned around only once, smiling and waving as the riders grew smaller in distance. Dolores buried her head on her husband's shoulder. He wrapped both arms around her as she began to shake with tears, letting all the pent-up emotion go.

'They'll be all right,' he whispered. 'Try not to worry about it, Mother.' He held her close so she could not see the tears welling up in his eyes, too.

★   ★   ★

'Will Keen, I'm sure surprised to see you back here in La Grange,' Sheriff John Skinner stood shaking hands with the trail scout. 'I hate to start off the conversation like this but I've got some bad news for you and the little lady here.'

'Bad news? We came back here to get married. Nothing's going to ruin that.'

192

'And I certainly don't want to either, but I have to tell you Burl Peet broke out of jail four days after you left. He's on the loose again, even though I got up a posse and tried to run him down. From what tracks we could follow, it looks like he headed east back up into the mountains. I hope I didn't wreck your wedding plans telling you this.'

Will's face turned dark with concern. 'How did he ever do that? I thought you had him locked up tight?'

'I did, until my deputy came over to the jail one evening with his dinner, while I was out of town for a few days. I warned him not to take any chances with Peet, but he got the drop on him anyway. Peet was on his bunk all curled up moaning he was too sick to eat but he wanted something to drink. When Frank unlocked the door and went in and tried to sit him up, he suddenly rolled over and came up swinging a heavy piece of wood from the bunk leg he'd worked loose. He clubbed Frank to the floor and beat him unconscious.

Then he dragged him up on the bunk, gagged him and handcuffed his hands together under it after tying his feet, and finally threw a blanket over him.

'I didn't find him until the next day when I got back in town. He took his gun belt out of my desk and one of my rifles, plus two boxes of cartridges.

'I hate to have to tell you all this, but it's better you hear it from me instead of someone else. You know how dangerous a snake Peet is, and he blames you for everything that's happened to him.'

Sarah's hand tightened in Will's. One glance at her face made it clear how scared and upset she'd suddenly become. Will knew he had to say something trying to calm her, and fast.

'We're going to get married as soon as I find a preacher. What Peet did doesn't make any difference to either of us.'

'I'd be glad to stand in as your best man, if you like.'

'That would be fine. I know both of us appreciate it, John.'

'Do you plan going back to the Willamette Valley, after you two tie the knot?'

'No, we don't. I mean to head east back over the mountains and across the high desert to Black Rock country. My mother used to own a ranch near there. I want to see what's left of it, if anything, after all these years.'

'But east is the way Peet went. You don't want to put the young lady and yourself in harm's way like that, do you? Why not wait until spring? Maybe by then Peet will either be caught or killed by someone else. His kind always ends up that way sooner or later.'

'What he's done isn't going to change Sarah and my plans. I had enough of that trying to get him here to jail. Now that he's on the loose again, I just better not run into him. If I do, there won't be any jail to it. I'll end it once and for all my way.'

The sheriff looked at both of them and decided to drop the subject. It was clear nothing he could say was going to change Will's mind. 'If you'll come with me, I'll take you two over to the church. Pastor Littlejohn should be there, and you'll walk out a married man. That's something I never thought I'd see.'

Skinner forced a quick smile, but behind his bushy handlebar moustache he was still worried about Will's insistence that he and Sarah ride east. He knew Will could handle a six-gun far better than most men — he'd done so all his life, and more than once. But he also knew that Burl Peet was cunning and vindictive, and if he got wind of the fact that Keen was anywhere in the same country as he was, the unrepentant killer would try to kill him any way he could.

Pastor Percy Littlejohn was a balding man with wire-rimmed glasses perched on a kind face that was always framed in an endless smile. He was devoutly certain that angels hovered among the big timber rafters of his church built by the sweat, toil and faith of his parishioners. Littlejohn exuded the goodness of a man who refused to believe anyone was soulless and could not be saved from the fiery furnace of hell. If Burl Peet walked into his church with six-gun blazing, the good pastor would have greeted him with a smile and message of redemption before being shot down himself. When Sheriff Skinner opened the door of the church and stepped inside, Littlejohn was replacing burned out candles in the foyer.

'Good day, sheriff.' He turned, eyeing Skinner, Keen and Sarah curiously. 'If you're coming in any further, I'll have to ask you and your friend to leave your weapons out here, please. I don't allow any guns inside God's house.'

Will and Skinner unbuckled gun belts without comment, placing them on a narrow table against the wall. 'Thank you. Now what can I do for you gentle-men?'

'We're here for a wedding. My friend Will Keen is marrying this lovely young lady.' The pastor's smile instantly grew larger.

'Well, then. Let's step inside so I can

begin the blessed ceremony and perform the nuptials. I assume there will be a congregation of friends and family coming soon?'

'No,' Skinner said. 'Just the three of us. I'm the best man.'

Littlejohn suddenly looked confused. It took a moment for him to recover. 'I see,' he pulled at his whiskerless jaw. 'I just thought so lovely a young lady would certainly want her family here to witness the joyous event.'

'They're too far away,' Will explained. 'Her mother and father are working on their new homestead in the Willamette Valley.'

'What a shame they cannot attend. Be that as it may, let's step into the main room. God will be your witness, and congregation too. I am certain he will revel in your joining.'

The interior of the church was cold and shadowed, with a faint smell of dust in the still air. The few high windows along the walls allowed in only minimal light. Littlejohn lit several candles behind the altar, before turning back to the three of them. 'Please hold hands while I begin to read, but first you'll both have to give me your full names.'

The service was brief and subdued. Regardless of the lack of well-wishers, a serene smile never left Sarah's face. Her eyes grew moist and her breath caught in her throat, when Will slipped her grandmother's ring on her finger.

'In the presence of God and all assembled, I now pronounce you, Will Keen, and you, Sarah Foot, husband and wife. You may now kiss your new bride,' the pastor instructed Keen, who stood frozen at the sudden order.

Will had never kissed Sarah in front of anyone before, and had only recently held her close, with her doing all the leading. He stood embarrassed and red-faced, while the pastor and sheriff waited for him to make the traditional kiss. All Will could muster was a brief peck on Sarah's cheek, before he thanked both men, then stepped back holding both her hands.

'Is there any cost for your service?' Skinner asked the black-frocked man.

'You can leave a donation for the church inside the box by the front door, if you wish. I know the Good Lord would look kindly upon you for your gift.'

'I'll do that,' the sheriff promised, and dropped a ten-dollar gold piece in the box as he was leaving. Percy Littlejohn looked after the odd threesome, talking to himself in a whisper.

'Strange couple,' he surmised. 'I hope the Good Lord looks after them. I have this troublesome feeling they're going to need his help and very soon. I don't know why, I just do.'

Outside on the street the sheriff shook hands with Will. 'I'd say congratulations are in order. Are you going to spend a few days here in town before leaving?'

'No,' Will shook his head. 'I have to buy a good packhorse and provisions, and as soon as I do we're riding out.'

'I'd try to talk you out of it if I

thought you'd listen to me.'

'I know. But it's something I have to do. You've been a good friend, John. Both Sarah and I appreciate your help standing in for us. Maybe we'll be coming back this way again in a year or two. Who knows for sure? I don't, at least not now.'

'I hope you do. The best of everything to both of you — and watch out, up in those mountains. I don't have to tell you why, so I won't.' The two men shook hands again, this time holding on a moment longer, neither sure if they'd ever see each other again.

Will and his new bride didn't leave La Grange that day as he'd hoped. Finding a big, strong packhorse took some doing, plus buying enough supplies for the long, difficult ride east. Inside the dry goods store Sarah stood at a glass-topped display case marvelling at a pearl-handled, double-barrel .22 calibre lady's derringer. The little pistol absolutely fascinated her.

'Will,' she called over her shoulder,

'would you come here for a moment?'

He turned from the list of goods he'd given the proprietor to join her. 'What is it, Sarah. Do you see something else we need?'

'I don't know about 'we', but I'd like to buy this pretty pistol, if we can afford it.'

He eyed the derringer. A slow smile came over his face. 'Sarah, that's almost a toy gun. It's a .22 calibre meant for birds or rabbits, things that size. It's not much good for anything else larger.'

'Maybe so, but I'd like to have something to carry. That big heavy Colt of yours is too much for me to handle, and this is more my size. I've never had a gun of my own before. Don't you think it's time I did? I am your wife, aren't I?'

Keen nodded. 'Yes, you certainly are that, and some kind of woman for sure. If you want it that bad I'll buy it for you.'

'Maybe I'll be able to shoot dinner for us!' She smiled, squeezing his hand.

At dawn the following morning Will and Sarah rode down the largely deserted streets of La Grange, leading a pack-horse loaded with provisions for the long ride over the mountains. Will cast a wary eye beyond the lower plateaus fronting the town. Farther back, higher up, the mountains were shrouded in grey curtains of swirling clouds. Through small openings he could catch a glimpse of peaks painted bone white in snow. The small canvas packer's tent he'd bought was the only protection he and Sarah would have from the onset of full blown winter weather.

He silently pondered the fact that he'd stubbornly insisted on riding east, straight into the teeth of snow country, and the prospect of more to come. He only hoped his trail skills would get his new wife and himself over the high country without any severe consequences. But although it left him edgy, he wasn't about to let it show.

The wagon trail he'd earlier brought the settlers down was now covered in snow. Over the next several days as he and Sarah rode higher, it only deepened, until their horses were wading knee deep through it. The thought that Burl Peet had ridden into this same high country never left Will's mind. He couldn't help wonder if Peet had made it all the way back to Cedarville, or if winter's icy grip hadn't killed him someplace along the trail. Bundled up as he and Sarah were in heavy jackets and gloves, and with wool scarves wrapped across their faces against the bitter bite of the wind, it seemed that the odds against Peet surviving had to be insurmountable.

How ironic, Will thought, that in the end nature's cruel hand would be the one to freeze the life out of the unrepentant killer. He had run to the mountains fleeing a posse, unprepared for high country winter. Surely he had to be lying dead someplace up ahead, buried under two feet of new snow by now.

★　★　★

And yet Peet's blind luck still held, fuelled by the same mindless vindictiveness that had kept him alive when he crossed the high desert with a festering bullet wound. Fleeing the posse led by John Skinner, he'd savagely whipped his horse higher into the mountains as the first big snowstorms of winter swept in. The safety of Cedarville still lay far ahead over the high pass miles away, when his horse finally collapsed from exhaustion and the freezing cold. Pulling Skinner's rifle out of its scabbard, he fired one shot and ended the animal's suffering — but not driven by compassion, because of compassion Peet had none. It was the meat he needed to stay alive, and quickly going to work he cut out what he could carry. When he had finished, he unbuckled the cinch strap and pulled off the saddle, then draped the saddle blanket over his shoulders as a wool cape. Next he cut loose the bit, thinking those long leather cheekpieces could come in handy for something.

He stood surveying the frozen land around him. Beyond a tall line of snow-clad pines he saw the outline of a rocky ridge not far away. Immediately he started for it through knee-deep snow. Reaching the rocky wall, he worked his way along its bottom until he found a shallow cave just large enough for him and his gear. Crawling into it, he took stock of his situation. At least for now he had shelter. He could start a fire from dead branches off the trees nearby for heat: above all he needed that to keep from freezing to death. He had meat to eat. Now if he could just come up with some way to travel on foot to Cedarville, once again fate would keep him alive. Burl's mouth twisted into a grim smile. He was alive, armed, and out of the weather. He might even live long enough to somehow face Will Keen again and kill him for sure if he ever got that chance.

For nearly two more weeks Peet struggled to survive in his stony hideout. When meat ran low he trudged back to the frozen horse carcass and hacked off more. Every day his mind kept searching for a way to travel, on foot, to reach Cedarville. He knew he couldn't live like this for ever — sooner or later he had to try to escape his snow-bound prison. One afternoon wading back to the cave, an idea suddenly dawned on him as he pushed through the tree-line. A thicket of bare winter willow brush stopped him dead in his tracks as he studied the bent branches. Maybe, he thought, he could cut several and bend them so they formed Indian snow shoes. He had pieces of leather off the reins for cross webbing, and could use part of the saddle blanket woven into them for foot holds.

The idea sent a bolt of anticipation like electricity coursing through him, and he spent the remainder of that day working feverishly to make a pair. He slept little that night, thinking about the following day. At the first hint of dawn he loaded the saddle bags with what meat he had left, filled his boots with horse hair, and secured the remainder of the saddle blanket over his shoulders to form a rough cape. Grabbing his rifle he stepped down as the first weak rays of winter sun lit the land in a million sparkling diamonds. Burl Peet was ready to escape the icy prison that had trapped him for so long. He took in a deep breath while squinting at the snowy high pass still far above. Somewhere over that top lay warmth, safety and food. He meant to stay on his feet to reach it, or die trying.

10

Three days of brutal foot slogging, climbing higher through deep snow, brought Peet to a stand of thick timber within sight of the final pass over the top. He staggered under snow-laden limbs, and collapsed head down, trying to catch his breath, shivering uncontrollably. His hands, wrapped in makeshift gloves, had lost all feeling. His face was numb, and his feet so cold he couldn't feel his toes any more. Pulling the saddle-bags over his shoulder, he dug for his last precious book of matches. He had to have a fire to thaw out and warm up before trying for the top. Gathering a small pile of sticks and branches, he tried lighting the first match. His hands shook so violently he could not ignite the pile of duff before the match burned out. He tried a second match and failed again. Panic and fear began to paralyse him. He had to think of some way to get control of his hands.

Unbuttoning his frozen coat, he shoved a hand under each armpit, praying it would work, eyes closed, teeth chattering. The third match flamed briefly to life. To shield it he leaned low over the tiny flame, keeping the wind out. A moment later a small puff of blue smoke meandered upwards, followed by a flickering flame as the little fire took hold and he fed it more pieces of wood. As the flames leapt higher he lay down, curling his body around the growing heat, steam rising off his clothes and boots.

He was still alive, still able to try for Cedarville, still fighting against all odds not to give up and die. Slowly his eyes closed as his body warmed up, and he gave in to sheer exhaustion, and the bitter cold. A moment later he collapsed into a deep sleep.

Peet awoke with a start. He didn't know how long he'd slept or what woke him, but something did. The small fire had burned down to a pile of warm ashes. He pulled himself up groggily, trying to rub some circulation back into his whiskered face. That's when he heard it again, a horse whinnying. A horse, up here? That was impossible. Rolling on to his knees he parted the branches, squinting out from under his snowy hideout to see two riders coming slowly closer. He couldn't believe his eyes. A horse could save him! Reaching for his rifle he studied the pair intently. Bundled in heavy clothes, their faces covered by scarves, he couldn't make out who they might be. The only thing he was sure of, it wasn't tall, lanky John Skinner, the La Grange sheriff. He'd seen enough of him to know that. But who else in their right mind would be riding up here in this frozen world of ice and snow, and why?

As the horses waded closer, Burl's jaw dropped and his mouth hung open. One of those horses was Will Keen's big animal Blue. A bolt of blind excitement coursed through Peet's body. After all

Keen had put him through — roping him in the saddle for days on end, then delivering him to jail in La Grange, with the likelihood of a long prison stay or even being hung — now he had the trail scout riding straight towards him, completely at his mercy. Burl shivered with emotion at the thought of it. Now he'd get even for all he'd been put through. The cards were dealt one last time, and he held all the aces.

Will reined Blue towards the big stand of timber with the intention of getting out of the wind and giving the horses a rest. He knew Sarah could use one too, even though she hadn't complained one single word about it. But twenty yards from the pines a lone figure suddenly burst out from under the limbs, screaming orders, levelling a rifle on him. It took a moment for Will to recognize the skeleton of a man with a shaggy beard and ragged clothes — and when he did, he couldn't believe Burl Peet was even still alive. Worse, Will knew even his fast hand with a six-gun couldn't beat a man with a rifle cocked and pointed at him.

'You two get your hands up and get down!' Burl screamed, relishing the moment, a wicked smile parting his whiskered face. 'Do it now or I'll kill both of you where you sit!'

Keen and Sarah eased down off the horses and stood side by side as Peet stepped closer. Suddenly Sarah realized who he was, her eyes widening in disbelief, her breath catching in her throat.

'You, Keen, left hand. Pull that hog leg of yours and toss it over there into the snow,' he motioned with the rifle. 'You make one wrong move and I'll kill you first!'

Will lifted the six-gun and threw it several feet away.

'Now that knife on your belt. Get rid of it too, same way. Then step away from those horses. You thought I'd be swinging from a rope by now, didn't you? You tried to kill me twice before, but I'm still alive. Now you're the one who's going down, and this time there won't be any re-deal. You get over here and get down on your knees, so you can't try anything smart. You,' he nodded to Sarah, 'step over here where I can get a better look at you.'

She took several halting steps up to the scarecrow of a man until he could reach up and begin to unwrap the scarf covering her face. Pulling it aside, he stepped back stunned and confused in disbelief. 'Well — I'll be damned. You're a girl, that Foot girl from the wagon train. But what are you doing up here with the likes of him?'

'We're married — we're going someplace far away. Will's not chasing you any more. Take one of the horses if you want, but let us go . . . '

'Married, you married yourself to this half breed?' He threw his head back laughing, but suddenly stopped. Grabbing Sarah by her jacket collar, he pulled her so close she was obliged to smell his foul breath and stare into his dark, beady eyes.

'Well girl, I'll tell you what: I got

some real news for you, and you better hear me real good. I'm about to make you a widow, then you and me are going to saddle up and ride to Cedarville. But the good part is you won't have to marry me, too. No siree. I'll just keep you busy cooking, cleaning up my cabin and keeping my bed warm at night. That'll be your new job, sweetie.'

He shoved her back so hard she lost her balance and fell into the snow, then he turned to Will. 'You know how long I've waited to finally kill you? I'd begun to think it would never happen, until you delivered yourself right up here to me. That was mighty neighbourly of you, and I'm going to give you one more chance to show how much of a sport I am because of it. You're already on your knees, so crawl over here to me and beg for your life. I just might spare you if you do. But the girl still goes with me, no matter what. And if I do decide not to kill you, I'll take both horses and leave you afoot just like I was. Winter will kill you anyway. Now go ahead.

Start crawling, I just gotta' see this. The great Will Keen crawling like a whipped dog!'

'You go to hell, Peet. That's where you're going anyway, no matter what happens up here.'

'All right, half breed. You called it. It's time you got yours — and remember before you die, I'm the man who gave it to you, and took your woman away, too!'

Burl lifted the rifle, taking careful aim through the steel sights, centring them on Keen's chest.

His finger was tightening on the trigger, when the sudden crack of the little double-barrelled derringer cut through the whistling wind. Peet's face twisted in agonizing pain, and he dropped the rifle, grabbing at his back. Taking a few stumbling steps forwards, he tried to stay on his feet — and then his legs buckled and he went down on his knees, his head dropping to his chest. Behind him Sarah slowly struggled to her feet, eyes wide with fear, still holding the little gun out in front of her, tight in both hands. Will ran forwards, grabbing Peet's rifle. Reaching Sarah, he took the gun from her trembling hands, then wrapped both his arms around her; she began to sob uncontrollably. When they both turned again, Burl Peet was face down in the snow.

'You are some kind of woman, Sarah Keen,' Will whispered, still holding her close. 'You and that little pistol you wanted so badly just saved both our lives.'

When Sarah regained control of herself Will slowly held her back at arms' length. 'We're going to be riding double, until we reach Cedarville.'

'Double, what for?' She wiped her eyes, still shivering from what she'd done.

'I'm roping Peet's body on your horse. I don't want it on our packer and supplies. They can do what they want with him once we reach town. I don't want anyone finding what's left of him out here come next spring, blaming me for it. There's always someone who makes up a story like that when they have no answers. We're not riding out of Cedarville, always having to look back over our shoulders. I'll settle all of it in town. Peet probably has friends who will try to stir up trouble. This way I'll end it before it even gets started. We've got enough in front of us without adding anything more to it.'

'If he'd shot one or both of us like he threatened, he would have left us out here,' she countered.

'Yes, I know that. But remember the good citizens of Cedarville were all ready to try and hang me because of Peet. I'm not going to give them any reason to try again. We're taking his body in with us.'

The three-horse caravan took three more days on the trail before they saw the snowy rooftops of town come into view ahead and below them. Will turned in the saddle and said to Sarah:

'When we get there let me do all the explaining. I don't want you to be involved in Peet's killing in any way if I can help it. There's no telling what some fool might come up with, especially if they learned you did the shooting. They might think we ambushed him instead of the truth.'

'I'm not afraid of that. We know what happened. Why hide it?'

'I know you're not afraid. But if there's any question about it — and there will be — I want them asking me, and not accusing you.'

The riders barely reached the first buildings in town before a small knot of men began following them on wooden sidewalks, pointing at the body roped over the saddle.

'Hey, isn't that the wagon scout that came through here sometime back?' one man asked. 'And what's he doing with a dead man behind him?' The group kept pace with the riders as more men joined them.

'Yeah, that's him all right,' another said. 'I'd know that big horse of his anyplace. But who's under that blanket, that's what I want to know.'

'Last time he came through town it led to trouble with almost a hanging party. Burl Peet tried to fire everyone up to do it. Remember that?' Several others nodded.

'We better find out what happened and who that is before someone goes off half cocked again,' the first man suggested.

Keen was well aware of the growing crowd of curious people pacing behind him. He heard some of the loud remarks shouted at him, but ignored them. Reaching the middle of town, he reined to a halt as the crowd, now several dozen strong, closed in around them. Will whispered for Sarah to stay in the saddle as he eased down on to the snowy street and walked back to her horse, carrying Peet's body, with all eyes riveted on him. The crowd suddenly grew quiet as he turned and looked at them. This was exactly what Will wanted. He'd make them wait a big longer, making the anticipation build so that he had his say first. His gloved hand began untying the ropes over the body, while he began to speak.

'This murderer tried to ambush my wife and myself four days out west of here. He broke out of jail in La Grange and fled a posse led by Sheriff John Skinner. I stopped him before he could kill anyone else. If anyone here wants what's left of him, he's all yours. I could have left him back in the snow for wolves or lions to finish off. Instead, I packed him all the way back here so there would be no doubt about what happened.'

Will slowly coiled up the loose rope and started to slide the blanket off the body. The instant it fell clear, the crowd reacted with shouts and even more questions.

'That's Burl Peet, or what's left of him!' One bystander exclaimed, pushing forwards to get a closer look.

'Looks like he finally got what was coming to him,' another added. 'He always was living on the edge. This time he fell off, for sure.'

'Wait a minute. How do we all know this story of Keen's is actually the truth? We only have his word for it. What we do know is Burl and him had bad blood between them, that's for sure.' A rough-looking man in the back of the crowd raised his voice and pushed forwards.

Will eyed the doubter. He expected someone might say something like this. After all, Cedarville did have its share of shady characters who never seemed to hold a job and didn't mind stepping over the law when they got the chance. Peet did have his sympathizers.

'It's true because I say it is,' Will shot back. 'And if anyone doubts what I say, then they can ride all the way over to La Grange and talk to Sheriff Skinner about it. He'll back up everything I've said. Anyways, I'm done explaining it. If anyone wants Peet's body, take it now, or I'll dump him right here on the street.'

Several men stepped up and pulled the body off Sarah's horse, then carried it up on the boardwalk while the rest of the crowd followed them, all talking at the same time. Will quietly motioned for Sarah to mount back up on her horse, and the moment she did they started away down the street towards the end of town without looking back. The sooner they left Cedarville behind, the better: Will knew that men left to their own designs, thoughts and unanswered questions were capable of suddenly fomenting dangerous confrontations. While they argued over what he'd told them, he and Sarah would have left the town as far behind them as possible; they had enough to face on the trail ahead without trying to outrun a group of rope-carrying vigilantes.

★   ★   ★

Nearly a full week of riding downhill left the town far behind, and lessening snow on the trail made it easier on both riders and horses. At night, when they pulled to a stop, Will put up the small canvas tent he'd purchased before leaving La Grange, so his new wife could stay at least a bit more comfortable and warm wrapped in her sleeping robe. Will had the habit of staying up late after Sarah turned in, feeding a small fire and watching their back trail. Always the thought that some of Peet's friends might try to catch up to them was never far from his mind. Even in death Peet's ghost seemed to haunt them.

Sometimes as he gazed at the icy stars on a bitter cold night, he couldn't help but wonder if his wild urge to return to the old ranch site of his boyhood made any sense at all. Why, after all these years, did it suddenly seem so important? Could it actually give him some peace of mind? There was only one way to find out, and in making the long ride east, he and Sarah were doing just that.

Riding out of the last foothills days later, Will pulled Blue around, studying the highlands they'd finally left behind. The peaks were lost in swirling clouds of icy white, and another big snow-storm was painting the land in deeper drifts. At least, he thought, Sarah and he had made it out before the trail became impassable until next spring's thaw. Now, the high desert stretched away before them. On the far side lay the endless alkali flats of the Black Rock Desert, with weeks more riding across its shimmering surface before the first rocky mountains rose on the far side, sheltering the little canyon home where his mother had fought so hard to eke out a living for so many years. The thought of it made his heart beat faster in his chest — but he couldn't help but wonder what his new wife would think when she first saw it in a land that seemed deserted, desolate and lonely. There was only one way to find out. He glanced at Sarah with a short question.

'Ready for this?'

'I am.' She smiled back bravely.

11

The snow-topped mountains finally fell far behind the two riders, but the bitter temperatures of winter still followed the Keens as they rode farther out into the high desert. The dry, dusty wagon road down which Will had led the twenty-three wagons months earlier, were now muddy, water-filled ruts with inch-thick ice on top. Ahead, high cliffs and rim rock tops were painted white in lacy designs of snow driven by freezing winds. But even through these bitter cold days and nights, Will was back in the land he knew so well and how to survive in it. Soon as they reached the land surrounded by those towering cliffs, that evening he reined Blue off the trail up a steep talus slope at the base of one tall monolith. Sarah wondered where he was going until she saw the dark opening to a large cave at the cliff bottom.

'We'll spend the night in here out of the wind. I'll get some sagebrush stumps for a fire after I unsaddle the horses. There's a small seep in the back of the cave where you can get some water if you want a drink or plan to cook something. It drips right out of solid rock into a stone bowl my ancestors left there a long time ago. You'll be comfortable and warm here tonight.'

Sarah looked at her new husband studying him intently before declaring, 'Is there anything you don't know or can't do? You always surprise me when I least expect it. That's one of the reasons I love you so much, Will.'

He stared back with just the flicker of a smile on his lips before answering. 'The ancient Paiute people knew every inch of this land and how to survive in it. They knew every hidden spring, cave and waterhole. They knew the desert animals that lived here and came to them to drink. They built rock blinds above them waiting to ambush deer and antelope when they came in. In some of these caves they buried their dead, too.'

'Did they in this one?'

'Yes, far back in the end I've found old bones, flint arrowheads, a few scraps of deerskin clothes. Does that bother you?'

'No it doesn't, as long as you're here with me. I meant what I said before. As long as we're together we can do anything and face anything we have to.'

He stepped up close, putting both hands on her shoulders and levelling a long, intense stare at her. 'I am two men, Sarah. You really only know one of me. I am a white man wearing white man's clothes, but my heart beats with the blood of my Paiute ancestors. Only a very few people know that, or even understand it.'

'I do know some of it, but it doesn't lessen my love for you, Will.'

He wrapped his arms around her, pulling her closer. 'Where I am taking you might make you take back those words. It's a place few white men have seen, or could live, close to the desert like it is. It's a lonely place far away from everything or anyone else.'

'I don't care where we go. We'll make it work no matter where it is.' She pulled his face down, kissing him lightly on the lips.

Each day the pair continued riding steadily southeast, surrounded by high cliffs whose faces continually changed colour as grey clouds scuttled by, changing the rays of the meagre winter sunlight. Several times in the late afternoon a cruel wind came up, sweeping in more clouds with dark bellies heavy with rain, announced by sudden flashes of thunder and jagged lightning. Will and Sarah would quickly ride for shelter under a rocky ledge or copse of junipers, waiting for the sudden downpour and wind to pass.

Half way across the high desert they reached a broad sagebrush valley surrounded by higher ridges and saddles along both sides. Starting into it they did not see a distant line of other riders several miles away, intently watching their progress. Black Antelope, wrapped in heavy animal skins, leaned forwards trying to make them out. It only took a moment for him to do so.

'It is my brother, Will Keen,' he pointed. 'The other one might be a woman. She is smaller.'

'If you are right, what is he doing back here in our land? He lives only with white men!' Running Coyote spoke, a tinge of insult in his voice.

'The only reason he would be here now is to go home. And we will follow him to be sure he gets there safely. He still carries the blood of our people in his veins.'

'You say he has a woman with him?' Diving Hawk asked.

'Yes, he must have taken a woman. If he has, that is good. It is time my brother has someone to warm his sleeping robe. He has always been alone. That is only half a man. With a good woman at his side, he becomes whole for the first time. We will follow him, but not let him know we are here.'

Long days in the saddle and freezing cold nights were finally rewarded weeks later when Will and Sarah pulled their horses to a halt at the last edge of the high desert plateaus. Downhill, stretching away as far as the eye could see, lay the bone-white expanse of the Black Rock Desert, shimmering under a clouded winter sun. Will eased Blue closer to Sarah. Standing in the stirrups he pointed across the alkali flats to the distant blue silhouette of low mountains on the far side marching across the horizon.

'I know you can't see it from here, but right there is the canyon where our old ranch was. That's where we're going, Sarah.'

She strained, squinting to make out the shadowed cleft. 'It still looks a long ways away. How long do you think it will take us, Will?'

'If winter rains haven't flooded the flats and we can get the horses across, I'd say we'll reach it in another two days.

If it's too muddy, we'll have to go around the far end and try to cross where it's narrower. That would take four or five.'

'I hope it's not that long. I'm anxious to get there and see it for myself.'

'So am I, Sarah,' his voice dropped off to a whisper. 'I've wondered about it for a while now, and I'm still not sure why.'

They started down the steep drop off with Will in the lead, Blue plunging through soft dirt and rocks, while Sarah's horse followed, straining to keep its feet. It took the remainder of that day to finally reach the bottom against the flats.

That evening they camped at the first edge of the immense playa under a beaver moon. They stood with their backs to a small fire in front of their tent, facing out into the endless expanse of desert. Through thin clouds above, the filtered glow of moonlight lit the desert in a ghostly glow. There was an unspoken reverence to this vast quiet desert that was hard to put into words. Sarah reached for Will's hand, clutching it tight. For a long time they stood side by side without speaking, under the magic spell of the Black Rock night. Finally Will said quietly, 'Let's turn in and get some sleep. Tomorrow we'll try going across.'

At dawn Will was up early, standing outside the little tent gazing across the playa to distant mountains on the far side. For once the winter skies had cleared, and it was a sparkling sunup. His thoughts of boyhood times over there crowded his mind with images of his mother, uncle and the Paiute Indian children he had grown up playing with. Would the long, difficult journey on which he'd taken his new wife find only the empty skeletons of his past? Could the ghosts he'd treasured as long lost friends really turn out to be demons instead? Sarah came to his side, bringing him back to reality.

'You're almost home, Will,' she whispered. 'I want to see this as much as you do. Let's get an early start. I'm too excited to waste time eating.'

He took in a long, deep breath

pulling her close. 'I need you now more than ever, Sarah. All of a sudden being so close has me questioning whether it was the right thing to do or not.'

'What do you mean, not the right thing? Of course it is. This is something you have to do, and not just for yourself, but for me, too. It's time you did something for yourself instead of everyone else, like you've done for so many years. Let's get the tent down and load the horses. It's a beautiful day and we can cover a lot of ground with an early start out there.' She eased around in front of Will resting her head on his chest. 'This is more to me than even your boyhood memories. It's the real start of our lives together and everything that comes after that. You cannot question it now. There's no turning back, Will.'

Crusted alkali crunched under the horses' hoofs as they rode out across the endless desert pan, with Will in the lead pulling the packer, and Sarah last in line. As the sun rose higher, the glistening white crystals seemed to come alive with a brilliant light of their own, causing Sarah to pull up her neck scarf to just under her eyes to keep back the blinding reflection. Up front, Will squinted hard until his eyes were only narrow slits, reining Blue steadily ahead towards the distant mountains without let-up. Hour after hour crept by, with only a line of hoofprints to show they had ever passed. In the wet spots their tracks sank deeper, slowly filling with milky-coloured water. Will glanced back at Sarah silently clinging to her horse without a word of complaint. Morning faded into high noon, then afternoon, the three tiny dots that were their horses the only thing to mar the endless expanse of the dazzling white desert pan. Hours later, near sundown, Will finally reined Blue to a stop, motioning Sarah up alongside him.

'We're over halfway across and making good time. If you can hold up we could keep going after dark. It's easier on the horses, and us too. What do you think? Is it too much for you?'

'No,' she lowered the scarf, shaking her head. 'Let's keep on. I'm all right. Just a little tired and thirsty.'

'Then let's take a break right now and have some water. The horses need it too.' He eased himself down and retrieved the canvas water bags from the packer, offering Sarah a drink. While she lifted the bag to her mouth, Will filled his hat with water for Blue, then the packer and Sarah's horse. After they'd had their fill they stood for a moment watching the last bit of sunlight blink out in the west. The first chill whisper of the evening breeze came dancing across the flats as the crescent rim of the beaver moon floated silently up behind the dark mountains, illuminating the desert pan in an eerie glow of its own. Back in the saddle they started again, as diamond-bright stars began dotting the deep velvet sky above.

Dawn was only a meagre grey slash in the eastern sky when Will made out the first dark shadows of mountains looming up ahead of them. He looked back, barely able to see Sarah, who with head down, was half asleep, still clinging to the saddle.

'Are you awake?' he called out.

She jerked upright. 'I . . . almost fell asleep, but I'm OK!'

'We're getting close to the mountains. The light will come faster now and we'll be able to see better.'

As the sky brightened, the jagged desert mountains showed Will that he had to angle further east to find the entrance to his canyon home. In another hour they reached the first flinty ground, finally leaving the vast alkali pan behind. They rode parallel with the steep foothills fronting higher ranges, their tops dotted with small stands of juniper and cedar. Will's eyes constantly searched ahead for the tell-tale sign of a few scattered Quaking Aspen trees that marked the canyon entrance to his boyhood home, and the small natural spring that fed them. Several canyons ahead he rounded a bend and saw the old, white-barked trees just ahead. A bolt of excitement coursed through his body. Twisting in the saddle he pointed ahead to Sarah, who quickly urged her horse past the packer and up alongside him.

'Do you see it, Will?' she asked excitedly. 'Is that it?'

'Yes, see those aspens? That's the entrance. It's the only canyon like it because of the water from the spring. Let's get up there.'

Reaching the canyon opening he pulled Blue to a sudden stop instead of kicking him ahead. The signs of an old trail were choked with weeds and brush. A sharp bend ahead hid the trail further.

'Why are we stopping?' Sarah asked, reaching over to grip Will's arm in support.

'I just want a minute to take it all in. The ranch house, if it's still there, is farther back past that bend. Maybe there's nothing left to see. Even this old road is nearly gone.'

'Come on. We'll ride in together.' She squeezed his arm. 'This is what we've both waited for.'

Another turn up the trail and the Black Rock desert disappeared from view behind them, while rocky mountains came steeply down on both sides. Suddenly a young forked-horn mule deer ran up the gravelly bank from the small creek where he'd gotten his morning drink. He froze, gawking at the riders for several seconds. One more look and he'd seen enough, and turned to pogo stick up the hillside out of sight, while a smile played over Will's face. They urged the horses ahead, further in.

At the back end the canyon opened up into a small, bowl-shaped amphitheatre. A scattering of small trees and tall brush seemed to hide the unmistakable outline of what was once a large, stone-walled ranch house. Will eased Blue closer, then reined him to a stop, slowly easing out of the saddle. Sarah did the same and came to his side. For several long seconds neither spoke, taking it all in; then she broke the silence.

'It must have been beautiful, Will. I

can only imagine what it once was.'

He nodded, and taking her hand, pushed through the weeds up to the opening in the stone wall that once held the front door. Another step and they were inside. The remnants of scattered furniture lay littered across the floor. Over on one wall the big stone fireplace his uncle had built still stood, except now it was filled high with the twigs and sticks of a wood rat's nest. Looking up, Will saw that the heavy, hand-hued timber rafters were still in place, but there were no shingles left on them. The entire house was open to the sky and weather. A few steps further in a cotton-tail rabbit scampered out from under a pile of debris, and ran out of the back door. Will stopped. Taking in a long, deep breath he surveyed it all, the ghosts of years gone by hovering in every wall.

'I guess I never expected this,' he said dejectedly.

'It's all still right here.' Sarah walked around in front of him and stared up into his eyes. 'We can rebuild all of it and make it a home again, just like your mother, you and your uncle did. It will be a new start for both of us, and our first home. Maybe the only home we'll ever want. Say you'll try, Will. I'll be right here by your side, helping you every step of the way.'

He didn't answer right away, his mind spinning with so many questions. Taking her hand they walked through the big room and out of the back door. The copse of white-barked aspen, their golden winter leaves flashing in the sun, was still there around the bubbling spring that gave the special canyon its unique supply of fresh, cool water.

Suddenly Sarah looked up and pointed at the canyon rim above them. A line of Paiute riders looked down on them, while Black Antelope raised his hand high, holding it there in greeting, until Will did the same. The ancient son of two different worlds had returned to the land of his birth. His blood brothers would never be far away if they were needed, to see it was so.

Will and Sarah Keen did rebuild the old ranch house, bringing it back to its former glory, and filled with the shouts of three young children who would grow up there, a boy and two little girls. Far across the Black Rock desert, up in the hills where wagon trains still passed through, the US Army would build an adobe-walled fort named Soldiers' Meadow, to supply and protect the new settlers from back east who hoped to find a new life of their own, too. Will saw the advantage of starting a horse ranch, selling his animals to the cavalry at the fort. Some of the wagoners also bought Will's horses to replace their worn-out animals after the brutal desert crossing, and the two thousand miles they'd come before it.

Will Keen's days of leading wagon trains, deadly showdowns and blazing gunfights were over. He had a new life, a new home, and a growing family to take care of. It was more than the famous trail blazer could ever have dreamed or hoped for. The man who lived in two worlds had made a world of his own, and had done so without losing his identity in either one. It was a feat that etched his name in the history books of the Wild West that once was. Winter winds still blow across the vast Black Rock desert to this very day, and an old Paiute legend has it that when twisting clouds form the filmy outline of a horse and rider racing across the sky, it's the spirit of Will Keen riding to greet his ancient ancestors, proving that spirits never die. And who am I to say otherwise?

We do hope that you have enjoyed reading this large print book.

Did you know that all of our titles are available for purchase?

We publish a wide range of high quality large print books including:
Romances, Mysteries, Classics
General Fiction
Non Fiction and Westerns

Special interest titles available in large print are:
The Little Oxford Dictionary
Music Book, Song Book
Hymn Book, Service Book

Also available from us courtesy of Oxford University Press:
Young Readers' Dictionary
(large print edition)
Young Readers' Thesaurus
(large print edition)

For further information or a free brochure, please contact us at:
Ulverscroft Large Print Books Ltd.,
The Green, Bradgate Road, Anstey,
Leicester, LE7 7FU, England.
Tel: (00 44) **0116 236 4325**
Fax: (00 44) **0116 234 0205**

The notorious bounty hunter known as Iron Eyes is tracking down his errant sweetheart Squirrel Sally, and his quest takes him all the way from Mexico to the forests of the West. However, unbeknown to him, unscrupulous men envious of his success in his profession are pursuing him with a view to a kill. Iron Eyes is unwittingly riding into the jaws of Hell itself and will not survive unless divine intervention comes to his rescue. The problem is, only the Devil knows where he's gone . . .

RETRIBUTION

Corba Sunman

Texas Ranger Chet Hallam stayed behind when his family moved to Kansas. Five years later he rides north to pay them a visit and discovers that his father, the county sheriff, left town a month ago to track down a gang of outlaws and never returned. But before he can set out, he's facing flying lead in a place where hired killers and renegades have the upper hand. It's time for Chet to deal out some justice of his own, while he searches for the truth about his missing father . . .

TO THE FAR SIERRAS

Will DuRey

When drifter Tom Belman's horse is stolen in the Texas panhandle, his pursuit of the young thief leads to an unfriendly reunion with a former soldier in his unit, Lou Currier, now sheriff of the small town of Ortega Point. A subsequent lynching compels Tom to find and return to her home an unknown woman who is also being sought by Currier's posse. But her investigation into the affairs of a local businessman upon returning to Ortega Point will put herself and Belman in grave danger . . .

THE HOLMBURY COUNTY SEAT WAR

K. S. Stanley

Who really was involved in the brutal massacre of a small village at the start of the American Civil War, and what became of them? In this bitter tale, the truth doesn't finally emerge until 1887, when good men turned bad fight ruthlessly to ensure that their town is elected as the Holmbury county seat.

LIGHTNING STRIKE!

Brent Towns

For five years it was thought the gunfighter known as Lightning Swift had crawled off into the desert to die after being wounded in a gun battle with Harley Mossop and his gang. How wrong everyone was. Someone shot the man who saved his life, and the gunfighter with the lightning-fast hands has returned from the grave, Colts blazing. He's mad and is not going to stop until the person responsible is planted in the ground. Then from the past looms a killer — Laredo Mossop, king of the fast-guns!

HUNTING HARKER

Greg Mitchell

When Ollie Harker's wagon fails to arrive at Logjam Creek, his employer hires Tom Parry and Durango Finch to find it. It appears that Harker has been killed by hostile Indians, but when a murder in town is linked to him, Harker's mission is revealed to be something more than routine freighting. The trail leads Parry and Finch to an illegal whiskey-running operation in which Logjam Creek's saloon owner is implicated — and the two hunters find themselves in deep peril when they come up against a ruthless gang of moonshiners . . .